CHILDREN'S THRIFT CLASSICS

Dracula

BRAM STOKER

Adapted by Bob Blaisdell
Illustrated by Thea Kliros

DOVER PUBLICATIONS, INC.
Mineola, New York

DOVER CHILDREN'S THRIFT CLASSICS

GENERAL EDITOR: STANLEY APPELBAUM
EDITOR OF THIS VOLUME: ADAM FROST

Copyright

Published in Canada by General Publishing Company, Ltd., 30 Lesmill Road, Don Mills, Toronto, Ontario.
Published in the United Kingdom by Constable and Company, Ltd., 3 The Lanchesters, 162–164 Fulham Palace Road, London W6 9ER.

Bibliographical Note

This Dover edition, first published in 1997, is a new abridgment of a standard text of *Dracula,* which was originally published by Archibald Constable & Co., London, in 1897. The introductory Note and the illustrations were prepared specially for this edition.

Library of Congress Cataloging-in-Publication Data

Stoker, Bram, 1847–1912.
Dracula / Bram Stoker ; abridged by Bob Blaisdell ; illustrated by Thea Kliros.
p.   cm. — (Dover children's thrift classics)
Summary: After discovering the double identity of the wealthy Transylvanian nobleman, Count Dracula, a small group of people vow to rid the world of the evil vampire.
ISBN 0-486-29567-2 (pbk.)
[1. Vampires—Fiction. 2. Horror stories.] I. Kliros, Thea, ill. II. Title. III. Series.
PZ7.S8745Dr   1997
[Fic]—dc21   96-49010
                                                CIP

Manufactured in the United States of America
Dover Publications, Inc., 31 East 2nd Street, Mineola, N.Y. 11501

Note

BRAM STOKER (1847–1912), the son of an Irish civil servant, spent much of his childhood as an invalid, during which time his mother entertained him with ghost stories and ghoulish legends. By the time he had entered Trinity College, however, he had recovered enough to become a star athlete as well as an honor student. Upon leaving college Stoker found work first in the civil service and then as a drama critic. He met the actor Henry Irving in 1876 and became his friend, traveling companion and manager, a position that he held for the next three decades. Despite this work, Stoker still found time to write, and he was able to complete a law degree during this time as well.

In 1897 *Dracula* was published, its story influenced perhaps by the tales that the author had heard from his mother as a child. Stoker went on to write seventeen books in all, but it is *Dracula* that has been the most popular, spawning hundreds of stage, television and film adaptations. The present volume faithfully retells the basic story of Stoker's classic, highlighting the adventure, suspense and terror of the original in a way that is sure to captivate young readers.

Jonathan Harker's Journal

3 May. Transylvania.—Left Munich at 8:35 P.M. on May 1st, arriving at Vienna early next morning. Having had some time when in London, I had visited the British Museum, and searched among the books and maps in the library regarding Transylvania; I saw that some foreknowledge of the country could be important in dealing with a nobleman of that country. Count Dracula lives in the midst of the Carpathian mountains, one of the wildest and least known portions of Europe. I read that every known superstition in the world is gathered in the Carpathians; if so, my stay may be very interesting. (I must ask the Count all about them.)

It was on the dark side of twilight when we got to Bistritz, which is a very interesting old place. Count Dracula had directed me to go to the Golden Krone Hotel, which I found to be old-fashioned. I was expected, for when I got near the door I faced an elderly woman in peasant dress. When I came close she bowed and said, "The Englishman?" "Yes," I said, "Jonathan Harker." An old man, who had followed her to the door, handed me a letter:

My Friend—Welcome to the Carpathians. I am anxiously expecting you. Sleep well tonight. At three tomorrow the coach will start for Bukovina. At the Borgo Pass my carriage will await you and bring you to me. I trust that your journey from London has been a happy one, and that you will enjoy your stay in my beautiful land.

Your friend,
DRACULA

4 May.—When I asked the hotel keepers if they could tell me anything of Count Dracula and his castle, both husband and wife made the sign of the cross, and said they knew nothing at all.

Just before I was leaving, the old lady came up to my room and said, "Must you go? Oh, young man, must you go? Don't you know what day it is?"

On my saying I did not understand what she meant, she went on: "It is the eve of St. George's Day. Do you not know that tonight, when the clock strikes midnight, all the evil things in the world will have their way? Do you know where you are going, and what you are going to?" She went down on her knees and begged me not to go.

"Thank you for your concern," I said, "but my business requires me to go."

She then rose and, taking a crucifix from her neck, offered it to me. I did not know what to do, for, as an English Churchman, I have been taught to regard such symbols as idolatrous. She put the rosary around my neck, and said, "For your mother's sake," and went out of the room. Whether because of the old lady's fear or the many ghostly traditions of this place, the crucifix is still round my neck.

5 May. The Castle.—When I got on the coach, the crowd round the inn door all made the sign of the cross and pointed two fingers towards me. I got a fellow passenger to tell me what they meant; he explained that it was a charm or guard against the evil eye. This was not very pleasant for me, just starting for an unknown place to meet an unknown man. Then our driver cracked his big whip over his four small horses, which ran abreast, and we set off on our journey.

The road was rugged, but still we seemed to fly over it with a feverish haste. Beyond the swelling green hills rose mighty slopes of forest up to the lofty Carpathian mountains. Right and left of us they towered, with the afternoon sun falling full upon them. As we wound our endless way, and the sun sank lower, the shadows of evening began to creep round us. As the evening fell, it began to get very cold. Sometimes the hills were so steep that, despite our driver's haste, the horses could

The road was rugged, but still we seemed to fly over it

only go slowly. I wished to get down and walk up the hills, as we do at home, but the driver would not hear of it. "No, no," he said, "you must not walk here; the dogs are too fierce." The only stop he would make was a moment's pause to light his lamps.

When it grew dark there seemed to be some excitement among the passengers, and they kept speaking to him, as though urging him to greater speed. Then through the darkness I could see a sort of patch of gray light ahead of us. The excitement of the passengers grew greater; the coach rocked on its springs, and swayed like a boat on a stormy sea. I had to hold on. The road grew more level, and we appeared to fly along. Then the mountains seemed to come nearer to us on each side; we were entering the Borgo Pass. As we flew along, the passengers, craning over the edge of the coach, peered into the darkness. It was evident that something very terrible was expected to happen, but though I asked each passenger, no one would explain. At last we saw before us the Pass opening out on the eastern side. There were dark, rolling clouds overhead, and in the air the heavy sense of thunder. I was now myself looking out for the carriage which was to take me to the Count. I expected to see the glare of lamps through the blackness, but all was dark. The only light was the rays of our own lamps. We could see now the sandy road lying white before us, but there was on it no sign of a vehicle. The passengers drew back with a sigh of gladness. The driver, looking at his watch, said to the others something which I could hardly hear: "An hour before the time!" Then, turning to me, he said:

"There is no carriage here. You are not expected after all. You will now come on to Bukovina, and return tomorrow." While he was speaking the horses began to neigh and snort. Then, among a chorus of screams from the passengers and a universal crossing of themselves, a carriage, with four horses, drove up behind us, overtook us, and drew up beside the coach. I could see from the flash of our lamps, as the rays fell on them, that the splendid horses were coal-black. They were driven by a tall man with a long brown beard and a tall black hat, which seemed to hide his face from us. I could only see the gleam of a pair of very bright eyes, which seemed red in the lamplight, as he turned to us. He said to the driver: "You are early tonight, my friend."

The man stammered, "The Englishman was in a hurry."

"That is why," the stranger said, "you wished him to go on to Bukovina? You cannot fool me, my friend; I know too much, and my horses are swift." As he spoke he smiled, and the lamplight fell on a hard-looking mouth, with very red lips and sharp-looking teeth. "Give me the gentleman's luggage," said the stranger, and my bags were handed out. Then I got out from the coach, and the Count's driver helped me with a hand which caught my arm in a grip of steel. Without a word he shook his reins, the horses turned, and we swept into the darkness of the Pass. I felt a strange chill, and a lonely feeling came over me, but a cloak was thrown over my shoulders, and a blanket across my knees, and the driver said: "The night is cool, sir, and my master the Count told me to take care of you." The carriage went at a hard pace straight along, then we made a complete turn and went along another straight road. It seemed to me that we were simply going over the same road again. By and by, I struck a match, and by its flame looked at my watch; it was within a few minutes of midnight.

Then a dog began to howl somewhere in a farmhouse far down the road—a long wail, as if from fear. The sound was taken up by another dog, and then another and another, till, carried on the wind which now sighed softly through the Pass, a wild howling began, which seemed to come from all over the country. At the first howl the horses began to strain, but the driver spoke to them soothingly, and they quieted down, but shivered. Then, far off in the distance, from the mountains on each side of us, began a louder and sharper howling— that of wolves—which affected both the horses and myself in the same way—for I had an impulse to jump from the carriage and run. After going to the far side of the Pass, the driver suddenly turned down a narrow roadway which ran sharply to the right.

Soon we were hemmed in with trees. Then it grew colder, and fine, powdery snow began to fall, so that soon we and all around us were covered with a white blanket. The keen wind still carried the howling of the dogs, though this grew fainter. The baying of the wolves sounded nearer and nearer, as though they were closing round on us from every side. I grew dreadfully afraid, and the horses shared my fear. The driver, however, was not in the least disturbed.

Suddenly, away on our left, I saw a faint flickering blue flame. The driver saw it at the same moment; he at once stopped the horses, and, jumping to the ground, disappeared into the darkness. After a few moments he returned, and we resumed our journey. I think I must have fallen asleep and kept dreaming of the incident, for it seemed to be repeated endlessly. Once the flame appeared so near the road, that even in the darkness around us I could watch the driver's motions. Then for a time there were no blue flames, and we sped onwards through the gloom, with the howling of the wolves around us.

I was afraid to speak or move. The time seemed endless as we swept on our way. We kept on ascending. Suddenly, I became aware of the fact that the driver was in the act of pulling up the horses in the courtyard of a vast, ruined castle, from whose tall, black windows came no ray of light, and whose broken, fort-like towers showed a jagged line against the moonlit sky.

When the carriage stopped, I got out, and the driver jumped down and took my bags, placing them on the

The wolves sounded as though they were closing round on us.

ground beside me. I stood before a great door, old and studded with nails, and set in a projecting doorway of stone. Then the driver jumped again into his seat and shook the reins; the horses started forward, and carriage and all disappeared down one of the dark openings.

I stood in silence, for I did not know what to do. There was no sign of bell or knocker. What sort of place had I come to, and among what kind of people? Was this a customary incident in the life of a lawyer's clerk sent out to explain the purchase of a London estate to a foreigner? Clerk! Mina, my fiancée, would not like that term. Lawyer—for just before leaving London I got word that my examination was successful, and I am now a full-blown lawyer!

I heard a heavy step approaching behind the great door, and saw through the chinks the gleam of a coming light. Then there was the sound of rattling chains and the clanking of massive bolts drawn back. A key was turned, and the great door swung back.

Within stood a tall old man, clean shaven save for a long, white moustache, and dressed in black from head to foot. He held in his hand a silver lamp, and he motioned me with his right hand, saying in excellent English, "Welcome to my house! Enter freely and of your own will!" He stood like a statue until I had stepped over the threshold, and held out his hand, which grasped mine; it seemed as cold as ice—more like the hand of a dead than a living man.

"Count Dracula?"

"I am Dracula; I bid you welcome, Mr. Harker. Come in, the night air is chill, and you must need to eat and rest." He insisted on carrying my bags himself along the hallway, and then up a winding stairway, and along another long hallway, on whose stone floor our steps rang heavily. At the end of this hallway he threw open a heavy door, and I rejoiced to see within a well-lit room in which a table was spread for supper, and in whose fireplace some fresh wood flamed and flared.

The Count halted, putting down my bags, closed the door, and, crossing the room, opened another door. This led into a small, eight-sided room lit by a single lamp, and seemingly without a window of any sort. Passing through this, he opened another door and motioned me to enter. Here was a large bedroom, well lighted and warmed with a fresh fire.

"You will need, after your journey, to wash up. When you are ready, come into the other room, where you will find your supper prepared."

After hastily washing, I went into the other room. The Count said, "I pray you, be seated and eat what you like. You will, I trust, excuse me that I do not join you, but I have dined already."

During the time I was eating, the Count asked me many questions as to my journey, and I told him all I had gone through. By the time I had finished my supper, I had had the chance to observe him and his odd features.

His face was strong and sharp, with a thin nose and strangely arched nostrils, and with a domed forehead, the hair growing scantily round the temples and richly elsewhere. His eyebrows were very large, almost meeting over the nose. The mouth, so far as I could see it under the heavy moustache, was rather cruel-looking, with oddly sharp white teeth; these teeth pushed out over his amazingly bright red lips. His ears were pale, and at the tops extremely pointed; the chin was broad and strong, and the cheeks thin. I also noticed his hands, which were broad with pudgy fingers. Strange to say, there were hairs in the center of the palm. The nails were long and fine, and cut to a sharp point.

When we were both silent for a time, I looked towards the window and saw the first dim streak of the coming dawn. Then we heard, as if from down below in the valley, the howling of many wolves. The Count's eyes gleamed, and he said: "Listen to them—the children of the night. What music they make!" Then he said, "But you must be tired. Your bedroom is all ready, and tomorrow you shall sleep as late as you will. I have to be away till the afternoon, so sleep well and dream well!" With a bow, he opened my bedroom door.

7 May.—It is again early morning, and I have rested and enjoyed the last twenty-four hours. I have not yet seen a servant anywhere, or heard a sound near the castle except the howling of wolves. Some time after I had finished my evening meal, I opened another door in the room and found a sort of library. The door opposite mine I tried as well, but it was locked.

While I was looking at the books, the door opened, and the Count entered. "I am glad you found your way in here, for I am sure there is much that will interest you. But alas! as yet I only know English through books."

"But, Count," I said, "you know and speak English very well!"

"I thank you, my friend, but I know that, did I move and speak in your London, none there are who would not know me for a stranger. You come to me not solely as agent of my lawyer, Peter Hawkins, to tell me about my new estate in London. You shall, I trust, rest here with me awhile, so that by our talking I may learn the English way of speaking."

Of course I said I was willing, and asked if I might come into the library when I chose. He answered, "Yes, certainly, you may go anywhere you wish in the castle, except where the doors are locked. There is a reason that doors are barred to you; our Transylvanian ways are not your English ways, and there shall be to you many strange things. From what you have told me of your experiences already, you know something of what strange things there may be."

I asked him then about the blue flames of the pre-ceding night, and why the coachman went to them. He explained that it was commonly believed that on a certain night of the year—last night, in fact, when all the evil spirits are supposed to have their way—a blue flame is seen over any place where treasure has been hidden.

After supper, we talked, as on the first night, of London until the crack of dawn. Here I lie in bed, having written of this day.

8 May.—There is something so strange about this place and all in it that I wish I were safe out of it, or that I had never come. If there were anyone to talk to I could bear it, but there is no one. I have only the Count to speak with, and I fear I am the only living soul within the place.

Suddenly I felt a hand on my shoulder.

I only slept a few hours when I went to bed, and, feeling that I could not sleep any more, I got up. I had hung my shaving mirror by the window, and was just beginning to shave; suddenly I felt a hand on my shoulder, and heard the Count's voice saying to me, "Good morning!" I was startled, for it amazed me that I had not seen him, since the reflection in the glass covered the whole room behind me. In being startled, I cut myself slightly. I turned to the glass again, and—though the man was close to me, and I could see him over my shoulder— there was no reflection of him in my mirror! But at the same time I saw the blood trickling over my chin, and, as I laid down the razor to look for a handkerchief, the Count's eyes blazed, and he made a grab for my throat! I drew away, and he said, "Take care how you cut yourself! It is more dangerous than you think in this country."

When I went into the dining room, breakfast was prepared, but I could not find the Count anywhere. It is strange that as yet I have not seen the Count eat or drink. He must be a very peculiar man! After breakfast I did a little exploring in the castle. I went out on the stairs and found a room looking towards the south. The view was magnificent. The castle is on the edge of a terrible cliff; a stone falling from the window would fall a thousand feet before touching anything. As far as the eye can reach is a sea of forests, with here and there a silver thread of a river. But when I had seen the view, I explored further; doors, doors everywhere, and all locked and bolted. In no place but the windows is there an exit. I am a prisoner!

A wild feeling came over me. I rushed up and down the stairs, trying every door and peering out of every window. I behaved much as a rat does in a trap. There is no use making my discovery known to the Count. He knows I am imprisoned; as he has done it himself he would only lie to me if I told him what I had found.

12 May.—Last evening the Count came to my room and asked me many questions about the English legal system, which I explained as well as I was able. Finally he asked, "Have you written your first letter to our friend, Mr. Peter Hawkins, or to any other?"

"I have not," I replied, "because as yet I have not seen any chance of sending letters to anybody."

"Then write now, my young friend," he said, laying a heavy hand on my shoulder. "Write to our friend, and to any other, and say, if it will please you, that you shall stay with me until a month from now."

"Do you wish me to stay so long?" I asked.

"I desire it much; I will take no refusal."

What could I do but bow in agreement? There was something in his eyes that reminded me that I was a prisoner, and I could have no choice.

"I ask you, my good young friend," he said, "that you will not speak of things other than business in your letters." Noticing his smile, with the sharp, canine teeth lying over the red underlip, I understood that I had better be careful what I wrote. So I decided to write only formal notes now, but to write fully to Mr. Hawkins in secret, and also to dear Mina, for to her I could write in shorthand, which would puzzle the Count.

When he left me I went to my room. After a little while, not hearing any sound, I came out and went up the stone stair to where I could look out towards the south. I gazed out over the beautiful view, bathed in a soft moonlight that made it almost as light as day. As I leaned from the window, my eye was caught by something moving a story below me, and somewhat to my left, where the Count's own room looked out.

What I saw was the Count's head coming out from the window. I was in terror when I saw him slowly emerge from the window and begin to crawl down the castle wall over that dreadful cliff, *face down,* with his cloak spreading out around him like great wings! At first I could not believe my eyes. But I kept looking, and I saw the fingers and toes grasp the corners of the stones and move downwards with great speed, just as a lizard moves along a wall.

What kind of man is this? I feel the dread of this horrible place overpowering me; I am in fear—in awful fear!

15 May.—Once more have I seen the Count go out in his lizard fashion. He moved downwards in a sidelong way, some hundred feet down, and to the left. He vanished into some hole or window. I knew he had left the castle now, and thought to use this chance to explore more than I had dared to as yet.

Taking a lamp, I tried all the doors within my room. They were all locked. At last, however, I found one door, through the hall and at the top of the stairway, which opened with a little pressure. I was now in a wing of the castle further to the right than the rooms I knew, and a story lower down.

Here I am, sitting at a little table in this unfamiliar room, and writing in my diary in shorthand.

Later: the morning of 16 May.—When I had written in my diary and had fortunately replaced the book and pen in my pocket, I felt sleepy. The Count had warned me not to fall asleep anywhere but in my own rooms, but I disobeyed him. I lay down on a couch and fell asleep. My dreams—would that they *were* dreams! For I cannot believe that what I saw did not happen.

I could see along the floor, in the moonlight, my own footsteps where I had disturbed the dust. In the moonlight I saw three young women. I thought at the time that I must be dreaming, for, though the moonlight was behind them, they threw no shadow on the floor. They came close to me and looked at me for some time, then whispered together. Two were dark and had large piercing eyes that seemed almost red. The other was fair, with wavy masses of golden hair and eyes like blue gems. I seemed somehow to know her face, but I could not remember how or where. All three had brilliant white teeth that shone like pearls against their ruby, moist lips. They whispered together, and then they all three laughed—a silvery, musical laugh.

"Go on!" said one of the dark ones to the fair. "You are first, and we shall follow."

The other added, "He is young and strong; there are kisses for us all."

The fair girl came and bent over me till I could feel her breath upon me. As she arched her neck she actually licked her lips, till I could see in the moonlight the moisture shining on the scarlet lips and on the red tongue. Lower and lower went her head, as the lips went below the range of my mouth and chin and seemed about to fasten on my throat. Then she paused, and I could feel the soft, shivering touch of the lips on the skin of my throat. I closed my eyes and waited— waited with a beating heart.

But at that instant, I opened my eyes and saw the Count's strong hand grasp the slender neck of the fair woman and draw her away, her blue eyes furious, her white teeth champing with rage. But the Count! His eyes were blazing. In a low whisper, he said, "How dare you touch him, any of you? How dare you cast eyes on him when I had forbidden it? Back, I tell you all! This man belongs to me! I promise you that when I am done with him you shall kiss him at your will. Now go! go! I must awaken him, for there is work to be done."

The horror of these words overcame me, and I passed out.

I awoke in my own bed. As I look around this room, I regard it now a sort of safe-haven, for nothing can be more dreadful than those awful women, who were—who *are*—waiting to suck my blood.

28 May.—There is a chance of escape, or at any rate of being able to send word home. A band of Gypsies has come to the castle, and is camping in the courtyard. I shall write some letters home, and shall try to get the Gypsies to have them posted.

I have written the letters. Mina's is in shorthand, and I simply ask Mr. Hawkins to contact her. To her I have explained my situation. I have given the letters; I threw them through the bars of my window with a gold piece and made what signs I could to have them posted. The man who took them pressed them to his heart and bowed, and then put them in his cap. I could do no more. I hurried back to the library and began to read.

The Count has come. He sat down beside me, and said in his smoothest voice as he opened the two let-

He calmly held letters and envelopes in the flame.

ters: "The Gypsy has given me these." He calmly held letters and envelopes in the flame of the lamp till they were burnt.

25 June, morning.—I must take action of some sort while the courage of the day is upon me. Action! It has always been at nighttime that I have been in danger or in fear. I have not yet seen the Count in the daylight. Can it be that he sleeps when others wake, that he may be awake while they sleep? If I could only get into his room! As the door is always locked, there is no way for me.

Yes, there is a way, if one dares to take it. Where his body has gone, why may not another go? I have seen him myself crawl from his window. Why should not I imitate him, and go in by his window? I shall risk it. At the worst it can only be death. God help me in my task! Goodbye, Mina, if I fall; goodbye, my faithful friend and second father, Peter Hawkins.

Same day, later.—I have made the effort, and God has helped me come safely back to this room. I went to the window on the south side, and at once got outside on the narrow ledge of stone which runs around the building on this side. The stones are big and roughly cut, and the mortar has by time been washed away between them. I took off my boots and looked down once, but after that kept my eyes away from below. I knew the direction and distance of the Count's window and made for it as well as I could. I did not feel dizzy—and it was only moments before I found myself standing on his window sill. I crawled down into the room. Then I looked around for the Count, but, with surprise and gladness, found the room was empty! The only thing I found was a great heap of gold in one corner.

At another corner was a heavy door. I tried it. It was open, and led through a stone passage to a circular stairway, which went steeply down. I went down, and at the bottom there was a dark, tunnel-like passage, through which came a deathly, sickly odor. As I went through the passage the smell grew worse. At last I pulled open a heavy door which stood ajar, and found myself in an old, ruined chapel, which evidently has been used as a graveyard. There were large wooden boxes filled with fresh earth. I went down within each of three marble tombs, and in two of these I saw nothing except fragments of old coffins and piles of dust. In the third, however, I made a discovery.

There, in one of the large boxes, of which there were fifty, on a pile of newly dug earth, lay the Count! He was either dead or asleep—for the eyes were open and stony—but the cheeks were full and the lips were red. There was no sign of movement, no pulse, no breath, no beating of the heart. I fled from the place and, leaving the Count's room by the window, crawled again up the castle wall. Regaining my room, I threw myself upon the bed and tried to think.

29 June.—I was awakened by the Count, who looked at me grimly and said, "Tomorrow, my friend, we must part. You return to your beautiful England, I to some work which may have such an end that we may never meet again. In the morning come the Gypsies. When they have gone, my carriage shall come for you, and shall bear you to the Borgo Pass to meet the coach from Bukovina to Bistritz."

"Why may I not go tonight?"

"Because, dear sir, my coachman and horses are away on a mission."

"But I could walk with pleasure. I want to get away at once."

"And your baggage?"

"I do not care about it. I can send for it some other time."

"Come with me then, my dear young friend." He led me down the stairs and along the hall to the door. He drew back the bolts and unhooked the heavy chains. As he began to draw it open, the howling of the wolves just outside the door grew loud and angry; their red jaws jutted in through the open door.

Leaping back, I cried out, "Shut the door! I shall wait till morning!"

In silence we returned to the library, and after a minute I went to my own room. The last I saw of Count Dracula was his kissing his hand to me.

When I was in my room and about to lie down, I thought I heard a whispering at my door. I went to it softly and listened. I heard the voice of the Count: "Back, back, to your own place! Your time is not yet come. Tonight is mine; tomorrow night is yours!" There was a ripple of laughter, and I threw open the door and saw there the three terrible women licking their lips. As I appeared they all joined in a horrible laugh and ran away.

30 June, morning.—These may be the last words I ever write in this diary.

To get the key that would let me out of this place, I scaled the wall again and entered the Count's room. He might kill me, but death seemed better than being a prisoner here. The room was empty. I went through the door in the corner and down the winding stair and along the dark passage to the old chapel.

The great box was in the same place, with the lid laid on it, but not hammered down. I knew I must find his body for the key, so I raised the lid, and laid it back against the wall; and there lay the Count, looking as if his youth had returned, for the white hair and moustache were changed to dark gray; the cheeks were fuller, and the white skin seemed ruby-red underneath; the mouth was redder than ever, for on the lips were trickles of fresh blood! It seemed as if he were gorged with blood. I shuddered as I bent over to touch him, but I had to search, or I was lost. I felt all over the body, but no sign could I find of the key.

In a rage I fled the room, and the passage door slammed shut after me, fastening itself somehow, and I cannot return.

There is in the passage below a sound of many tramping feet—the Gypsies come to take this terrible load to England!—and the crash of boxes with their freight of earth. There is a sound of hammering.

Hark! in the courtyard and down the rocky way the roll of heavy wheels, the crack of whips, and the chorus of the Gypsies as they pass into the distance.

I am alone in the castle with the awful women! I shall not remain; I shall try to scale the castle wall farther than I have yet attempted. I may find a way from this dreadful place. And then away for home! Away to the quickest and nearest train! Away from this cursed spot, from this cursed land, where the devil and his children still walk with earthly feet!

Goodbye, all! Mina!

Mina Murray's Journal

24 July. Whitby.—Lucy, my dearest friend, recently engaged to Arthur Holmwood, met me at the station, and we drove up to the house in which she and her mother have rooms. This is a lovely place. Right over the harborside town is the ruin of Whitby Abbey. Between it and the town there is another church, round which is a big graveyard, all full of tombstones. This is—to my mind—the nicest spot in Whitby, for it lies right over the town, and has a full view of the boats and harbor. There are walks, with seats beside them, through the graveyard, and people go and sit there all day long, looking at the beautiful view and enjoying the breeze. I shall come and sit here very often myself and work.

26 July.—I am unhappy about Lucy and about Jonathan. I have not heard from him. That is not like him. Then, too, Lucy, although she is so well, has lately taken to her old habit of walking in her sleep. Mrs. Westenra, her mother, tells me that her husband, Lucy's father, had the same habit; that he would get up in the night and dress himself and go out. Arthur is coming up here very soon—as soon as he can leave town, for his father is not very well, and I think dear Lucy is counting the moments till he comes. She wants to take him up to the graveyard cliff and show him the beauty of the sea.

8 August.—Lucy was restless all night, and I, too, could not sleep. There was a fearful storm, and it made me shudder. Lucy got up twice and dressed herself. Fortunately, each time I awoke in time and managed to undress her without waking her, and got her back to bed.

Early in the morning we both got up and went down to the harbor to see if anything had happened in the night. Somehow I felt glad that Jonathan was not on the sea last night, but on land. But, oh, is he on land or sea? Where is he, and how?

I think it will be best for Lucy to go to bed tired out physically, so I shall take her for a long walk by the cliffs to Robin Hood's Bay and back. She ought not to need to sleep-walk then.

11 August, 3 A.M.—No sleep now, so I may as well write. I am too agitated to sleep. We have had such an adventure, such an agonizing experience. I awoke, and sat up in bed, with a horrible sense of fear upon me. The room was dark, so I could not see Lucy's bed; I went across and felt for her. The bed was empty. I lit a match and found that she was not in the room. The door was shut, but not locked, as I had left it. I feared to wake her mother, who has been ill lately, so I threw on some clothes and got ready to look for her. I ran downstairs and looked in the sitting room. Not there! Then I looked in all the other open rooms of the house. Finally I came to the hall door and found it open. I took a big, heavy shawl and ran out. The clock was striking one as I was in the street, and there was not a soul in sight. I ran along, but could see no sign of her. At the edge of the cliff above the pier I looked across the harbor to the east cliff, in the hope or fear of seeing Lucy in our favorite seat. There was a bright full moon, with heavy, black, driving clouds, which threw the whole scene into light and shade as they sailed across. For a moment or two I could see nothing, as the shadow of a cloud went over St. Mary's Church and all around it. Then as the cloud passed I could see the ruins of the abbey coming into view, and the church and graveyard became visible. There, on our favorite seat, the silver light of the moon struck a half-reclining white figure. It seemed to me that something dark stood behind the seat where the white figure shone, and bent over it. What it was, whether man or beast, I could not tell. I flew down the steep steps to the pier and along by the fish-market to the bridge, which was the only way to reach the east cliff. The time and distance seemed endless. When I got almost to the top I could see the seat

There was something bending over the half-reclining figure.

and the white figure. There was undoubtedly something, long and black, bending over the half-reclining white figure. I called in fright, "Lucy! Lucy!" and something raised a head, and from where I was I could see a white face and red, gleaming eyes. Lucy did not answer, and I ran on to the entrance of the graveyard. As I entered, the church was between me and the seat, and for a minute or so I lost sight of her. When I came in view again the cloud had passed, and the moonlight struck so brilliantly that I could see Lucy half-reclining with her head lying over the back of the seat. She was quite alone.

When I bent over her I could see that she was still asleep. Her lips were parted, and she was breathing in long, heavy gasps. As I came close she put up her hand in her sleep and pulled the collar of her nightdress close around her throat. I flung the warm shawl over her, and drew the edges tight round her neck, for I dreaded her getting a deadly chill from the night air, dressed as she was in her filmy nightgown. I fastened the shawl at her throat with a big safetypin, but I must have been clumsy and pinched or pricked her with it, for she put her hand to her throat and moaned. I put my shoes on her feet, and then began very gently to wake her. Finally she opened her eyes and awoke. She trembled a little, and clung to me. We got home without meeting a soul.

When we got in, and had said a prayer of thankfulness together, I tucked her into bed. Before falling asleep, she asked me not to say a word to her mother about her sleep-walking adventure. I promised, and Lucy is sleeping soundly.

Same day, noon.—All goes well. Lucy slept till I woke her and the adventure of the night seems not to have harmed her; indeed, she looks better this morning than she has done for weeks. I was sorry to notice my clumsiness with the safetypin hurt her. It might have been serious, for the skin of her throat was pierced. I must have pinched up a piece of loose skin and pinned it, for there are two little red points like pinpricks, and on the band of her nightgown was a drop of blood. She said she did not even feel it.

13 August.—A quiet day. I woke in the night, and found Lucy sitting up in bed, still asleep, pointing to the window. I got up and, pulling aside the blind, looked out. It was moonlight, and beautiful. But between me and the moonlight flitted a large bat, coming and going in great whirling circles. Once or twice it came quite close, but was, I suppose, frightened at seeing me, and flitted away across the harbor towards the abbey. When I came back from the window, Lucy had lain down again and was sleeping peacefully.

14 August.—Lucy had a headache and went early to bed. I saw her asleep, and went out for a little stroll myself; I walked along the cliffs, and was sad, for I was thinking of Jonathan. When coming home—it was then bright moonlight—I took a glance up at our window, and saw Lucy's head leaning out. Her eyes were shut; she seemed fast asleep, but by her, seated on the window sill, was something that looked like a good-sized bird. I ran upstairs, but as I came into the room, she was moving back to her bed, fast asleep, and breathing heavily. She was holding her hand to her throat, as if to protect it from the cold. I did not wake her, but tucked her in. I have taken care that the door is locked and the window fastened.

She looks so sweet as she sleeps; but she is paler than usual, and there is a drawn look under her eyes which I do not like. I fear she is fretting about something.

17 August.—I have not had the heart to write. No news from Jonathan, and Lucy seems to be growing weaker, while her mother is slowly dying. I do not understand Lucy's fading away as she is doing. She eats well and sleeps well, and enjoys the fresh air, but all the time the roses in her cheeks are fading, and she gets weaker day by day; at night I hear her gasping for air. I keep the key of our door always fastened to my wrist at night, but she gets up and walks about the room, and sits at the open window. Last night I found her leaning out when I woke up, and when I tried to wake her I could not; she was in a faint. I trust her feeling ill may not be from that unlucky prick of the safety pin. I looked at her throat just now as she lay asleep, and the tiny wounds seem not to have healed. They are still

I looked at her throat as she lay asleep.

open, and, if anything, larger than before, and the edges of them are faintly white. They are like little white dots with red centers. Unless they heal in a day or two, I shall insist on the doctor seeing them.

18 August.—I am happy today, and write sitting on

the seat in the graveyard. Lucy is ever so much better. Last night she slept well all night. The roses seem to be coming back already to her cheeks, though she is still sadly pale.

19 August.—Joy, joy, joy! although not all joy. At last, news of Jonathan. The dear fellow has been ill in Budapest; that is why he did not write. I am to leave in the morning and go over to help nurse him, and to bring him home. My journey is all mapped out, and my luggage is ready. I copy out the letter I received from Sister Agatha at the hospital in Budapest:

12 August

Dear Madam,

I write by desire of Mr. Jonathan Harker, who is not strong enough to write, though recovering. He has been under our care for nearly six weeks, suffering from a brain fever. He wishes me to send his love and to say that he is sorry for his delay. He will need a few weeks' rest in our hospital, but will then return.

I must also say something more to you, my dear. Mr. Harker has told me all about you, and that you are shortly to be his wife. All blessings to you both! He has had some fearful shock—and his ravings have been dreadful: of wolves and blood; of ghosts and demons. Be careful with him always that there may be nothing to excite him of this kind for a long time to come. We should have written long ago, but we knew nothing of his friends. He came in the train from Klausenberg. Be assured that he is well cared for. He is truly getting well, and I have no doubt he will in a few weeks be himself.

I pray to God for many happy years for you both.

With sympathy and blessings,
SISTER AGATHA

Lucy Westenra's Journal

Hillingham, 24 August.—I must imitate Mina, and keep writing things down. Then we can have long talks when we do meet again on her return from nursing and marrying Jonathan Harker. I wish she were with me again, for I feel so unhappy. Last night I seemed to be dreaming again just as I had at Whitby. I can remember nothing, but it is all dark and horrid to me. When Arthur, my dear love, came to lunch, he looked quite upset when he saw me, and I hadn't the spirit to try to be cheerful. I wonder if I could sleep in Mother's room tonight.

25 August.—Another bad night. Mother did not want me to sleep in her room; she is not well. I tried to keep awake, but when the clock struck twelve it waked me from a doze, so I must have been falling asleep. There was a scratching at the window, but I remember no more. I suppose I must then have fallen asleep. More bad dreams. I wish I could remember them. This morning I am horribly weak. My face is too pale, and my throat pains me.

Letter from Arthur Holmwood
to Dr. John Seward

London, 31 August

My dear Jack—

I want you to do me a favor. Lucy is ill; she is getting worse every day. I have asked her if there is any cause.

I am sure there is something preying on my dear girl's mind. I told her I should ask you to see her, and though she refused at first—I know why, old fellow, as you also had wished her to be your wife—she finally consented. It is for her sake, old friend, and I must ask you to help. You are to come tomorrow. I must go to London to be with my father, who is, I fear, dying. Write me as soon as you can with a report on her health.

ARTHUR

Letter from Dr. Seward to Arthur Holmwood

2 September

My dear old fellow—

With regard to Miss Westenra's health, I hasten to let you know that she is not physically ill. At the same time, I am not by any means satisfied with how she looks. She is somewhat pale, but I could not see the usual signs of lack of blood. I have come to the conclusion that her illness must be mental. She complains of difficulty in breathing at times, and of dreams that frighten her, but regarding which she can remember nothing.

I am in doubt about her, so have done the best thing I know of; I have written to my old friend and professor, Van Helsing, of Amsterdam, who knows as much about strange diseases as anyone in the world. I have asked him to come over. He is one of the most advanced scientists of our day. I shall see Miss Westenra tomorrow again.

Yours always,
JOHN SEWARD

Dr. Seward's Journal

7 September.—Van Helsing and I were shown up to Lucy's room. If I was shocked when I saw her yesterday, I was horrified when I saw her today. She was ghastly, chalkily pale; the red seemed to have gone even from her lips and gums, and the bones of her face stood out; her breathing was painful to see or hear. Van Helsing's face grew set as stone. Lucy lay motionless, and did not seem to have strength to speak, so for a while we were all silent. Then Van Helsing beckoned to me, and we went out of the room. "My God!" he said, "this is dreadful. There is no time to be lost. She will die for want of blood. There must be a transfusion of blood at once. Is it you or me?"

"I am younger and stronger, professor. It must be me."

"Then get ready at once. I am prepared."

Just then, at the hall door, came in Arthur, Lucy's fiancé and my dear friend. He rushed up to me, saying, "Jack, I was so anxious. My father is somewhat better, so I hurried here to see Lucy for myself." Then turning to my older friend, he said, "Are you Dr. Van Helsing? I am so thankful to you, sir, for coming."

"Sir," said Van Helsing, "you have arrived in time. She is bad, very bad. But you are to help her. You can do more than anyone."

"What can I do?" said Arthur. "My life is hers."

"She wants blood," explained Van Helsing, "and blood she must have or die. My friend John and I are about to perform a transfusion of blood—to transfer from the full veins of one to the empty veins of another. John was to give his blood, as he is the more young than me, but you are now here; you are better than us."

"I would die for her," said Arthur.

"Good boy!" said Van Helsing. "You will be happy that you have done all for her you love. Come!"

Van Helsing noticed a red mark on her throat.

We all went up to Lucy's room. Van Helsing gave her a drug, and then we performed the operation. As the transfusion went on, something like life seemed to come back to poor Lucy's cheeks. When it was all over, I could see how much Arthur was weakened.

Dr. Van Helsing adjusted Lucy's pillow, and as he did so he noticed a red mark on her throat. He quietly gasped, but he said nothing, and told me to take Arthur away.

When I returned to the room, I asked the professor, "What do you make of that mark on her throat?" Just over the jugular vein were two punctures, not large; there was no sign of disease, but the edges were white and worn-looking.

"I must go back to Amsterdam tonight," said Van Helsing. "There are books and things there which I want. You must remain here all the night, and you must not let your sight pass away from her. You must not sleep. I shall be back as soon as possible."

8 September.—I sat up all night with Lucy. She never stirred, but slept on and on in a deep, tranquil sleep. There was a smile on her face. A telegram came from Van Helsing, stating he was leaving by the night train and would join me early in the morning.

9 September.—I was pretty tired and worn out when I got to Lucy's. For two nights I had hardly had a wink of sleep.

Lucy looked me sharply in my face and said, "No sitting up tonight for you. I am quite well again. You can lie on the sofa next door to my room. If I want anything I shall call out, and you can come to me at once." I agreed, for I was "dog-tired."

10 September.—I was aware of the professor's hand on my head, and started awake. "And how is our patient?" he asked.

Together we went into her room. As I raised the blind, the morning sunlight flooded the room. I heard the professor gasp, and a deadly fear shot through my heart. "God in Heaven!" he exclaimed.

There on the bed lay poor Lucy, more horribly white than ever. Even her lips were white, and her gums seemed to have shrunken back from the teeth. Van Helsing felt her heart and, after a few moments of suspense, said, "It is not too late. But all our work is undone; we must begin again. I have to call on you for the transfusion this time, my friend John."

Without a moment's delay we began the operation. No man knows, till he experiences it, what it is to feel his own blood drawn away into the veins of the woman he loves. For, of course, though she is engaged to Arthur, I love her still. Van Helsing will sit up with her tonight.

11 September.—This afternoon I went over to Hillingham. I found Van Helsing in excellent spirits, and Lucy much better. Shortly after I arrived, a big parcel came for the professor. He opened it and showed us a great bundle of white flowers. "These are for you, Miss Lucy," he said. "These are medicines."

She threw them down, saying, with laughter, "Oh, professor, you are pulling a joke! These flowers are only garlic!"

"But there is much good in these common flowers. You must obey me, if only for the sake of others."

First, he fastened up the windows in her room and latched them; next, taking a handful of the flowers, he rubbed them all over the sashes, all over the doorway, and round the fireplace.

He then began to make the necklace of garlic which Lucy was to wear. The last words he said to her when she got into bed for the night were: "Take care you do not remove your necklace, eh? No matter the smell, do not tonight open the window or door."

"I promise," said Lucy.

As we left the house, Van Helsing said, "Tonight I can sleep in peace. Tomorrow in the morning we come together to see the pretty miss, so much more strong for my 'spell.'"

13 September.—Van Helsing and I arrived at Hillingham at eight o'clock. It was a lovely morning. Lucy's mother greeted us, and told us, "You will be glad to know that Lucy is better. I was anxious about the dear child in the night, and went into her room. She was sleeping soundly—but the room was awfully stuffy. There were a lot of horrible, strong-smelling flowers about everywhere; she had actually a bunch of them round her neck. So I took them all away and opened a bit of the window to let in fresh air. You will be pleased with her, I'm sure."

As she spoke, I watched the professor's face and saw it turn gray. The instant she walked away, he raised his hands over his head in despair. "Come," he said, "come, we must act. We must fight the devils." Together we went up to Lucy's room.

Once again I drew up the blind.

"As I expected," he murmured. As he spoke he took off his coat and rolled up his shirt-sleeve. Again the transfusion operation; again some return of color to her pale cheeks.

Later he went to tell Mrs. Westenra that she must not remove anything from Lucy's room; that the flowers were medicine, and that her breathing them was part of the cure. Then he said he would watch over her this night and would send me word when to come.

18 September.—This morning I received a telegram, delayed twenty-four hours by a misdirection, from Van Helsing in Antwerp, telling me to be by Lucy's side— *last night!* A whole night lost! We know by bitter experience what may happen in a night.

I drove at once to Hillingham and met Van Helsing running up the avenue. When he saw me, he gasped out, "How is she? Did you not get my telegram?"

I answered that I had only got his telegram early in the morning, and had not lost a minute in coming here. We entered the house and rushed upstairs. We opened Lucy's door.

How shall I describe what we saw? On the bed lay two women, Lucy and her mother. The window was broken. The flowers which had been round Lucy's neck were around her mother's, and Lucy's throat was bare, show-

On the bed lay two women, Lucy and her mother.

ing the two little wounds we had noticed before, but looking horribly white and mangled. The professor bent over the bed, listening for Lucy's heartbeat. Her mother, clearly, was already dead. The professor leaped to his feet, crying, "It is not yet too late!—But what are we to do now? Where are we to turn for help? We must have another transfusion of blood soon, or that poor girl won't last an hour."

"What's the matter with mine?" This was spoken by Quincey Morris, yet another of my friends and, as well, one of Lucy's former suitors. He had come because of a telegram from Arthur, which read: "Have not heard from Dr. Seward for three days. Cannot leave my ill father. Send me word how Lucy is. Do not delay."

Van Helsing greeted the American, and said, "A brave man's blood is the best thing on this earth when a woman is in trouble."

We took her into another room, and once again we went through the ghastly operation. Though plenty of blood went into her veins, her body did not respond to the treatment as well as on the other occasions, and she slept heavily and breathed with difficulty.

We examined her poor mother, who had died from a heart attack. We sent a messenger for the undertaker.

When Lucy woke, her eyes lit on Van Helsing and then on me too, and she smiled. Then she looked around the room and shuddered; she gave a loud cry, and put her hands before her face. We both understood what that meant—that she had realized or remembered her mother was dead. We told her that either or both of us would now remain with her all the time, and that seemed to comfort her. Towards dusk she fell into a doze.

19 September.—All last night she slept poorly, and was somewhat weaker when she woke. The professor and I took turns watching. In the morning she was hardly able to turn her head, and she did not want to eat. While asleep, her open mouth showed the pale gums drawn back from the teeth, which looked longer and sharper than usual. In the afternoon she asked for Arthur, and we telegraphed for him.

When he arrived, less than a day after the death of

his father, it was nearly six o'clock, and the sun was setting. When he saw her, Arthur was choking with emotion. In his presence, she was more lively than earlier, but then soon fell asleep. I fear that tomorrow she will die.

20 September.—I relieved Van Helsing in his watch over Lucy. She lay quite still, and I looked round the room to see that all was as it should be. I could see that the professor had carried out in this room his purpose of using the garlic. She was breathing with trouble, and her open mouth showed the pale gums. Her teeth seemed even longer and sharper than they had been in the morning. In particular, her canine teeth looked longer and sharper than the rest. I sat down by her, and soon she was restless. There came a dull flapping or beating at the window. I went over to it softly, and peeped out by the corner of the blind. There was full moonlight, and I could see that the noise was made by a huge bat, which wheeled round and every now and again struck the window with its wings. When I came back to my seat I found that Lucy had moved slightly, and had torn away the garlic flowers from her throat. I replaced them as well as I could, and sat watching her.

Soon she woke, and I gave her food, as Van Helsing had ordered. But she was not hungry and ate little. At six o'clock Van Helsing came to relieve me. Arthur had fallen into a doze, and he had let him sleep on. When the professor saw Lucy's face he said, "Draw up the blind; I want light!" Then he bent down and examined her face carefully. He removed the flowers from her throat, and as he did so, he exclaimed, "My God!"

I bent over and looked, too; the wounds on the throat had absolutely disappeared. Van Helsing turned to me and said, "She is dying. It will not be long now. Wake that poor boy Arthur, and let him come and see the last."

I went to the dining room and waked him. He was dazed for a moment. I told him as gently as I could that both Van Helsing and I feared that the end was near. He covered his face with his hands, while his shoulders shook with grief.

He covered his face with his hands.

When we came into Lucy's room, she opened her eyes and, seeing him, whispered, "Arthur! Oh, my love, I am so glad you have come!" He was stooping to kiss her, when Van Helsing held him back. "No, not yet! Hold her hand; it will comfort her more."

So Arthur took her hand and knelt beside her, and then gradually her eyes closed, and she sank to sleep.

Her breathing grew difficult, her mouth opened, and the pale gums, drawn back, made the teeth look longer and sharper than ever. In a sort of sleep-waking, she opened her eyes, which were now dull and hard at once, and said in a soft, enticing voice, "Arthur! Oh, my love, I am so glad you have come! Kiss me!" Arthur bent over eagerly to kiss her, but at that instant Van Helsing swooped upon him and, catching him by the neck with both hands, dragged him back.

"Not for your life!" he said, "not for your living soul and hers!" And he stood between them.

Arthur was so taken aback that he did not for a moment know what to do or say. I kept my eyes on Lucy and saw a fit of rage pass over her face; the sharp teeth champed together. Then her eyes closed, and she breathed heavily.

Very shortly after, she opened her eyes in all their softness and, putting out her pale, thin hand, took Van Helsing's large hand; drawing it to her, she kissed it.

Then the professor turned to Arthur, and said to him, "Come, take her hand in yours, and kiss her on the forehead."

Arthur did so, and then Lucy's eyes closed. Her breathing became heavy again, and all at once it ceased. "It is all over," said Van Helsing. "She is dead!"

I took Arthur by the arm and led him away to the drawing-room, where he sat down and sobbed.

I went back to the room and found Van Helsing looking at poor Lucy. Some change had come over her body. Her brow and cheeks had recovered some of their flowing lines; even the lips had lost their paleness. I stood beside Van Helsing and said, "Ah, well, poor girl, there is peace for her at last. It is the end!"

He turned to me, and said, "Not so! Alas, it is only the beginning."

When I asked him what he meant, he answered, "We can do nothing as yet. Wait and see."

The funeral was arranged for two days from then, so that Lucy and her mother might be buried together. I attended to all the formalities, as Arthur had had to return to attend to his father's funeral.

Before turning in tonight, Van Helsing and I went to look at poor Lucy. All Lucy's loveliness had come back to her in death; I could not believe my eyes that I was looking at a corpse.

The professor looked grave, and said, "Tomorrow I want you to bring me a set of surgical knives."

"Must we make an autopsy?" I asked.

"Yes and no. I want to operate, but not as you think. Let me tell you now, but not a word to another. I want to cut off her head and take out her heart. Ah! you are a surgeon and so shocked! Oh, but I must not forget, my dear friend John, that you loved her. I would like to do it tonight, but for Arthur I must not; he will be free after his father's funeral tomorrow, and he will want to see her—to see it. Then, when she is coffined for the next day, you and I shall come when all are asleep. We shall unscrew the coffin lid and shall do our operation, and then replace all, so that none know but ourselves."

"But why do it at all? The girl is dead!"

"Friend John, there are things that you know not, but that you shall know, though they are not pleasant things. Were you not amazed and horrified when I would not let Arthur kiss his love—though she was dying—and snatched him away with all my strength? Yes! And yet you saw how later she thanked me with her hand pressing mine. Yes! Well, I have good reason now for all I want to do. You have for many years trusted me; trust me now. Friend John, there are strange and terrible days before us. Let us not be two, but one, so that we work to a good end. Will you not have faith in me?"

I took his hand, and promised him.

21 September.—Arthur arrived at five o'clock and visited the death chamber. Poor fellow! He looked sad and broken. He had just lost his father and his fiancée!

"Oh, Jack! Jack!" he cried out to me. "What shall I do! There is nothing in the wide world for me to live for."

I comforted him as much as I could. Then I said softly to him, "Come and look at her."

God! how beautiful she was. Every hour seemed to add to her loveliness. It frightened and amazed me. Arthur trembled, saying in a whisper, "Jack, is she really dead?"

I assured him that it was so.

He took her hand in his and kissed it, and bent over and kissed her forehead.

I slept on a sofa in Arthur's room that night. Van Helsing did not go to bed at all. He went to and fro, patrolling the house, and was never out of sight of the room where Lucy lay in her coffin, covered with wild garlic flowers.

Jonathan Harker's Journal

24 September.—I thought I would never write in this diary again, but the time has come. Mina and I have returned to London, a happily married couple. I had thought I was over my nightmare at Castle Dracula. But when I got home last night, Mina told me the tragic news of Lucy's death, and of having met Professor Van

Helsing this afternoon. She showed him my diaries, and he informed her that all I wrote down was true. Now that I *know* it was no nightmare, I am not afraid, even of the Count. He has succeeded, I discover, in getting to London. Van Helsing, however, is the man to unmask him and hunt him out, if he is anything like Mina says.

Dr. Seward's Journal

24 September.—Vån Helsing returned, and he thrust last night's newspaper into my hand. "What do you think of that?" he asked, pointing out a paragraph about children being kidnapped by a strange woman, who bit them in the neck.

"Whatever it is that injured her," I answered, "has injured them."

"Do you mean to tell me, friend John, that you have no idea as to what poor Lucy died of; not after all the hints given? You do not let your eyes see, nor your ears hear. Do you not think that there are things which you cannot understand, and yet which are; that some people see things that others cannot? There are always mysteries in life. Can you tell me why there are bats that come at night and open the veins of cattle and horses and suck dry their veins; how in some islands of the Western seas there are bats which hang on the trees all day, and that when the sailors sleep on deck, because it is hot, the bats flit down on them, and then—then in the morning they are dead men, white as even Miss Lucy was?"

"Good God, professor!" I said. "Do you mean to tell me that Lucy was bitten by such a bat, and that such a thing is here in London in the nineteenth century?"

"I want you to believe in things that you cannot. If you are willing to understand, you have taken the first step to understanding. You think then that those small holes in the children's throats were made by the same that made the holes in Miss Lucy's?"

"I suppose so," I answered.

"Then you are wrong; they were made by Miss Lucy!"

I was angry, and rose up as I said, "Dr. Van Helsing, are you mad?"

"I wish I were. My friend, it was because I wished to be gentle to you, for I know you loved that so sweet lady, that I went so far round to tell you so simple a thing. It is hard to accept so sad a truth. Tonight I want to prove it. Will you come with me? I want us to spend the night, you and I, in the graveyard where Lucy lies."

At about ten o'clock we started away. It was then very dark. We met very few people. At last we reached the wall of the graveyard, which we climbed over. With some difficulty—for it was very dark—we found the tomb of Lucy and her mother. The professor, who had a key, opened the creaky door, and we went in, closing the door after us. Then he took out a matchbox and a piece of candle. The funeral flowers now hung lank and dead about the tomb.

Van Helsing held his candle so he could read the coffin plates, and found Lucy's. Then he took out a screwdriver.

"What are you going to do?" I asked.

"To open the coffin. You shall yet be convinced." Right away he began taking out the screws, and finally lifted off the lid, showing the casing of lead beneath. The sight was almost too much for me. I actually took hold of his hand to stop him. He only said, "You shall see," and took out a tiny saw. He sawed down a couple of feet along one side of the lead coffin, and then across, and up the other side. Taking the edge of the loose lead, he bent it back towards the foot of the coffin and, holding up the candle into the opening, motioned to me to look.

I drew near and looked. The coffin was empty! It was certainly a surprise to me, but Van Helsing was unmoved. "Are you satisfied now, friend John?"

"What do you think of that?" he asked.

"I am satisfied that Lucy's body is not in the coffin, but that only proves one thing."

"And what is that, friend John?"

"That it is not there."

"That is good logic," he said, "but how do you account for it not being there?"

"Perhaps a body-snatcher," I suggested. "Some of the undertaker's people may have stolen it."

"Ah well," said the professor, "we must have more proof. Come with me."

He put on the coffin lid again, blew out the candle, and opened the door, and we went out. Behind us he closed the door. Then he told me to watch at one side of the graveyard while he would watch at the other. I took up my place behind a tree, and he behind one at the far side.

Just after I had taken my place, I heard a distant clock strike twelve, and in time came one and two. I was cold, and angry with the professor for taking me on such an errand. Suddenly, as I turned round, I saw something like a white streak, moving between two dark trees at the side of the graveyard farthest from the tomb. I hurriedly went toward the dim white figure as it flitted in the direction of the tomb. The tomb itself was hidden by trees, and I could not see where the figure disappeared.

And then I found the professor coming from the other side. "Are you satisfied now?" he asked.

"No."

He shook his head with disappointment and said, "Tomorrow afternoon, then, I shall show you the coffin again."

25 September.—Outrageous as it was to open a leaden coffin, to see if a woman dead nearly a week were really dead, it now seemed the height of folly to open the tomb again, when we knew that the coffin was empty. Van Helsing led me to the tomb this afternoon, opened it, and we went inside. He walked over to Lucy's coffin, bent over, and again forced back the leaded cover; then a shock of surprise shot through me.

There lay Lucy, seemingly just as we had seen her the night before her funeral. She was, if possible, more beautiful than ever, and I could not believe that she was dead. Her lips were redder than before, and her cheeks were rosy.

"Are you convinced now?" said the professor.

"Are you convinced now?" said the professor. He pulled back her lips and showed the white teeth. "See, see, they are even sharper than before. With this and this"—and he touched one of the canine teeth and that below it—"the little children can be bitten. Do you believe now, friend John?"

"I do not know."

"She was bitten by the vampire when she was in a

trance, sleepwalking. In a trance she died, and in a
trance she is Un-Dead, too. We must kill her in her
sleep. I shall cut off her head and fill her mouth with
garlic, and I shall drive a stake through her body."

It made me shudder to think of, and yet I was beginning to shudder at this being, this Un-Dead, as Van
Helsing called it.

"I have been thinking," he said, "and have made up
my mind as to what is best. If I simply followed my
instincts, I would do now what has to be done. But
instead, tomorrow night we will meet with Arthur and
the American, Quincey."

So we locked the tomb and came away, and climbed
over the wall of the graveyard, and drove back.

27 September, morning.—Last night, Arthur, Quincey,
and I came into Van Helsing's room at my home in the
hospital; he told us all what he wanted us to do. "I want
your permission," he said, "to do what I think good
tonight. It is much to ask. But I want you to promise me,
so that afterwards, though you may be angry with me
for a time, you shall not blame yourselves."

"That's frank, anyway," broke in Quincey. "I don't
quite see your drift, but I trust you."

"I thank you, sir," said Van Helsing.

"I agree as well," said Arthur. "And now that we have
agreed, may I ask what it is we are to do?"

"I want you to come with me in secret to the graveyard at Kingstead."

Arthur's face fell, as he said, "Where poor Lucy is
buried?"

"We shall enter her tomb," said Van Helsing.

"Professor, are you serious?" said Arthur.

Van Helsing nodded and said, "And then we shall
open the coffin."

Arthur was outraged, and exclaimed, "How dare you!"

"Would it not be better to hear what I have to say?" said Van Helsing. "Miss Lucy is dead; is it not so? Yes! Then there can be no wrong to her. But if she is not dead—"

Arthur jumped to his feet. "Good God!" he cried. "What do you mean? Has she been buried alive?"

"I did not say she was alive, my child; I mean to say she might be Un=Dead."

"Un-Dead!"

"There are mysteries which men can only guess at, and this is one. But I have not finished my proposal. May I cut off the head of dead Miss Lucy?"

"Heavens and earth, no!" cried Arthur. "Van Helsing, what have I done to you that you should torture me? What did that poor girl do that you should want to cast such dishonor on her grave? Are you mad? I have a duty to protect her from such outrage!"

Van Helsing answered, "Arthur, now Lord Godalming, I, too, have a duty, a duty to others, a duty to you, a duty to the dead, and, by God, I shall do it! All I ask you now is that you come with me, that you look and listen. But do not go forth in anger with me. I have never had so heavy a task as now. Why should I give myself so much labor and sorrow? I have come here from my own land to do what I can of good. I gave to your Lucy the blood of my veins."

Arthur was much moved and took the old man's hand, saying in a broken voice, "Oh, it is hard to think of, and I cannot understand, but at least I shall go with you and wait."

It was just a quarter before midnight when we got into the graveyard over the low wall. The night was dark, with occasional gleams of moonlight between the heavy clouds. We all kept close together, with Van

Helsing in front as he led the way to the tomb. He unlocked the door and entered first. The rest of us followed, and he closed the door. He then lit a lantern and pointed to the coffin.

He said to me, "You were with me here yesterday. Was the body of Miss Lucy in that coffin?"

"It was."

He took his screwdriver and again took off the lid of the coffin. Arthur looked on, very pale; when the lid was removed he stepped forward. Van Helsing forced back the lead cover, and we all looked in and recoiled.

The coffin was empty!

For several minutes no one spoke a word.

"Is this your doing, professor?" said Quincey.

"I swear to you that I have not removed her. Two nights ago, my friend Seward and I came here. I opened that coffin, which was then sealed up, and we found it as now, empty. We then waited, and saw something in white come through the trees. The next day we came here in daytime, and she lay there. Did she not, friend John?"

"Yes."

"Wait, all of you, with me outside, unseen and unheard; things much stranger are yet to be." Van Helsing opened the door, and we filed out.

In silence we took the places assigned to us, close round the tomb but hidden from the sight of anyone approaching. There was a long spell of waiting, and then from the professor came a "Sh-sh-sh-sh!" He pointed; far down the walkway we saw a white figure advance—a dim white figure, which held something at its chest. The figure stopped, and a ray of moonlight fell on a dark-haired woman, dressed in grave clothes. We could not see her face, for it was bent over what we saw to be a child. There was a pause and a sharp little cry.

We were starting forward, but the professor's warning hand, seen by us as he stood behind a tree, kept us back; as we looked, the white figure moved forwards again. It was now near enough for us to see clearly. My heart grew cold as ice, and I could hear the gasp of Arthur, as we recognized the features of Lucy Westenra. It was she, yet she was changed. Van Helsing stepped out, and we all advanced too; the four of us ranged in a line before the door of the tomb. Van Helsing raised his lantern and focused it on Lucy's face; we could see that her lips were red with fresh blood, and the stream had trickled over her chin onto her death-robe.

We shuddered with horror. When Lucy—I call the thing that was before us Lucy because it bore her shape—saw us she drew back with an angry snarl, such as a cat gives; then her eyes ranged over us. Lucy's eyes were full of hell-fire, instead of the pure, gentle eyes we knew. At that moment, I knew she had to be killed. As she looked us over, her eyes blazed with light, and she smiled with hunger. Oh, God, how it made me shudder! With a careless motion, she flung to the ground the child that up to now she had clutched to her chest, growling over it as a dog growls over a bone. The child gave a sharp cry, and lay there moaning. Arthur groaned at that, but when Lucy advanced to him with outstretched arms and a wicked smile, he fell back and hid his face in his hands.

"Come to me, Arthur," she said. "Leave these others and come to me. My arms are hungry for you. Come, and we can rest together. Come, my husband, come!"

Arthur seemed under a spell; moving his hands from his face, he opened wide his arms. She was leaping for them, when Van Helsing sprang forward and held between them his little golden crucifix. She recoiled from it, and with a face full of rage dashed past him.

Van Helsing held between them his crucifix.

We all looked on in horrified amazement as we saw
the woman, with a body as real at that moment as our
own, pass in through a crack of the closed door where
hardly a knife could have gone.

Van Helsing lifted up the little boy she had bit, examined him, nodded to us, and said, "Come now, my
friends; we can do no more till tomorrow. We shall
return tomorrow afternoon; there is more to do. As for
this child, he is not much harmed, and we shall leave
him where the police will find him."

They all came home to the hospital with me, where I
provided rooms for them.

27 September, night.—A little before noon we three—
Arthur, Quincey, and myself—called for the professor.
We all wore black clothes. Van Helsing, instead of his little black bag, had with him a long leather one. We followed the professor to the tomb. He unlocked the door,
and we entered, closing it behind us. Then he took from
his bag a lantern, which he lit. When he again lifted the
lid of Lucy's coffin, we all looked—Arthur trembling—
and saw that the body lay there in all its death-beauty.
But there was no love in my heart, nothing but hatred
for the foul thing which had taken Lucy's shape without
her soul. Arthur said to Van Helsing, "Is this really
Lucy's body, or only a demon in her shape?"

"It is her body, and yet it is not. But wait a while, and
you shall see her as she was, and is."

She seemed like a nightmare of Lucy as she lay there;
the pointed teeth, the bloodstained mouth seeming like
a devilish imitation of Lucy's purity.

Van Helsing took out his surgical knives and a round
wooden stake, some three inches thick and about three
feet long. One end of it was hardened by charring in a
fire, and was sharpened to a fine point. With this stake
came a heavy hammer. When all was ready, he said,
"Before we do anything, let me tell you this; when the
Un-Dead become such, they become immortal; they
cannot die, but must go on age after age adding new
victims; for all that die from the Un-Dead become themselves Un-Dead, and prey on others. Friend Arthur, if
you had met that kiss before Lucy died, or again, last
night when you opened your arms to her, you would in
time, when you had died, have become another Un-
Dead. The career of this unhappy dear lady is but just
begun. Those children whose blood she sucked are not
as yet so much the worse, but if she lives on, Un-Dead,
more and more they will lose their blood, and by her
power over them they will come to her. But if she dies

now, then they will be fine; the tiny wounds on their throats will disappear, and they will go back to their playing, unknowing ever of what has been. But the most blessed thing of all, is that when this now Un-Dead is made to rest as the true dead, then the soul of the poor lady whom we love shall again be free; she shall be able to take her place with the other angels. It will be a blessed hand for her that shall strike the blow that sets her free."

We all looked at Arthur. He stepped forward, and said bravely, "My true friend, tell me what I am to do."

Van Helsing laid a hand on his shoulder and said, "Brave lad! This stake must be driven through her. It will be fearful—but it will be only a short time. Take this stake in your left hand, ready to place the point over the heart, and the hammer in your right. Then when we begin our prayer for the dead, strike in God's name, that all may be well with the dead that we love, and that the Un-Dead pass away."

Arthur took the stake and the hammer, and when Van Helsing began to read the prayer, Arthur struck with all his might. The thing in the coffin writhed, and a hideous screech came from the opened red lips. The body shook and quivered; the sharp white teeth champed together. And then the quivering stopped, and finally the thing lay still. The terrible task was over.

The hammer fell from Arthur's hand. He would have fallen had we not caught him. After the few minutes it took him to recover, we looked again in the coffin, and there lay no longer the foul thing that we had so dreaded, but Lucy as we had seen her in her life, with her face of sweetness and purity. One and all we felt the holy calm that lay over her.

Van Helsing came and said to Arthur, "And now, dear lad, am I not forgiven?"

"Forgiven!" cried Arthur, "God bless you that have

given my dear one her soul again." Arthur now bent and kissed Lucy's face, and then we sent him and Quincey out of the tomb; the professor and I sawed the top off the stake, leaving the point of it in the body. Then we cut off the head and filled the mouth with gar-

He said, "This stake must be driven through her."

lic. We sealed the leaden coffin, screwed on the coffin lid, and gathering up our belongings, came away. When the professor locked the door, he gave the key to Arthur.

Outside, the air was sweet, the sun shone, and the

birds sang. Before we all left the graveyard, Van Helsing said, "Now, my friends, one step of our work is done, one the most difficult for our feelings. But there remains a greater task: to find out the creator of all this and to stamp him out. I have clues which we can follow, but it is a long task, and there is danger in it, and pain. Shall you not all help me?"

We each in turn took his hand and promised to help.

Then the professor announced, "Two nights from today you shall meet with me and two others that you do not know as yet; I shall be ready to show you my plans."

When he and I arrived at the hospital, Van Helsing found a telegram waiting for him:

"Am coming up by train. Jonathan at Whitby. Important news.—MINA HARKER."

The professor was delighted. "That wonderful Madam Mina," he said. "She arrives, but I must return for two days to Amsterdam. She must stay with you here at the hospital. You must meet her at the station and bring her here." Then he told me of a diary kept by Jonathan Harker and gave me a typewritten copy of it, and also Mrs. Harker's diary. "Take these," he said, "and study them. What is here told may be the beginning of the end to you and me and many another; or it may sound the death knell of the Un-Dead who walk the earth."

Mina Harker's Journal

30 September.—Jonathan joined us this morning, having received my telegram to come. We all met in Dr.

Seward's study as a sort of committee. Professor Van Helsing took the head of the table. He made me sit next to him on his right, and asked me to act as secretary. Jonathan sat next to me. Opposite us were Arthur (that is, Lord Godalming), Dr. Seward and Quincey Morris.

The professor said, "Having read each other's diaries and participated in lengthy discussions, we are all now acquainted with the facts of this case. So I think that I should tell you something of the kind of enemy with which we have to deal, so we then can discuss how we shall act. There are such beings as vampires; some of us have seen that they exist. We must work, so that other poor souls do not perish. The vampire does not die like the bee after he stings once. He is only stronger, and being stronger, he has yet more power to do evil. The vampire which is among us is as strong as twenty men; he is cunning, for he has lived for ages; all the dead that he can come close to are at his command; he is a devil without a heart; he can direct a storm, or fog, or thunder; he can command animals: the rat, owl, bat, and wolf; he can grow and become small; he can at times disappear. How then are we to destroy him? If we fail here, it is not mere life or death. It is that we shall become like him; that we from then on shall become foul things of the night like him—preying on the bodies and souls of those we love best. To us forever would the gates of Heaven be shut. But can we avoid this duty to try to destroy him? For me, I say no. What do you say?"

My husband looked in my eyes and I in his. There was no need for speaking between us. "I answer for Mina and myself," he said. "We shall help."

"Count me in, professor," said Quincey.

"I am with you," said Lord Godalming, "for Lucy's sake."

"Can we avoid this duty to try to destroy him?"

Dr. Seward simply nodded.

The professor stood up to speak. "Well, you know what we have to contend against, but we, too, are not without strength. We have on our side a power denied to vampires: we have science; we are free to act and think; and the hours of the day and night are ours equally. Now let us consider the limitations of vampires in general, and this one in particular. All we have to go on are traditions and superstitions. The vampire has been known everywhere, in every time: in old Greece, old Rome, old Egypt; he lives now in India, in France, in China, in Iceland. The vampire lives on; he fattens on the blood of the living. What is more, we have seen among us that he can even grow younger. But he cannot go on without blood; he does not eat otherwise. Even Jonathan never saw Dracula eat.

"A vampire does not throw a shadow; he does not reflect in a mirror. He can be a wolf or a bat. He can come in a mist. He can come on the rays of the moon as dust. He can see in the dark. He can do all these things, yet he is not free. He is even more a prisoner than a madman in his cell. He cannot go anywhere he likes; he who is not of nature has yet to obey some of nature's laws—why, we do not know. He may not enter anywhere unless there is someone of the household who asks him to come in, though afterwards he can come as he pleases. If he is not at the place where he means to go, he can only change shapes at noon or at exact sunrise or sunset. Then there are things which so afflict him that he has no power, such as garlic, or a crucifix. A branch of wild rose on his coffin will keep him there; a sacred bullet fired into the coffin will kill him so that he is truly dead; and as for the stake through his heart, we know of that already, and of the cut-off head that gives him rest. We have seen it with our own eyes.

"So when we find the home of this man-that-was, we can confine him to his coffin and destroy him, if we obey what we know. And now we must settle what we shall do. We know from Jonathan that from the castle to Whitby came fifty boxes of earth, all of which were delivered from the boat to Carfax, the ruined estate next door to this very hospital. We also know that some of these boxes have been moved. It seems to me that our first step should be to find out whether all the rest remain in Carfax, where we shall look today. And now for you, Madam Mina, this night is the end until all be well. You are too precious to take any risks. We men shall act all the more free if you are not in danger."

They set out for Carfax, and told me to go to bed and sleep—as if a woman can sleep when those she loves are in danger!

Jonathan Harker's Journal

1 October, 5 A.M.—Having climbed over the wall from the hospital to the Carfax estate, we took our way to the house. When we got to the porch the professor opened his bag and took out a lot of things, which he laid on the step, sorting them into four little groups, one for each of us. Then he spoke: "My friends, we are going into a terrible danger. We must guard ourselves from his touch. Keep this near your heart"—as he spoke he lifted a crucifix—"put these flowers round your neck"—here he handed out wreaths of withered garlic blossoms, and finally he gave us portions of holy wafers. We were all armed with guns and knives as well, and we strung electric lamps over our chests to keep our hands free as we searched.

We pressed on the door, the rusty hinges creaked, and it slowly opened. We closed the door behind us, turned on our lamps, and proceeded. I had the feeling that there was someone else among us. We kept looking over our shoulders at every sound and new shadow.

The whole place was thick with dust. The floor was seemingly inches deep in it, except where there were recent footsteps. The walls were fluffy and heavy with dust, and in the corners were masses of spiderwebs. On a table in the hall was a ring of keys, with labels on each. After a few minutes we found the way to the chapel. We selected the proper key and opened the door; none of us expected such a stagnant and foul odor as we found.

Under ordinary circumstances, such a stench would have ended our mission, but after a few moments we

In a few moments the chapel was filled with rats.

went on and examined the place. There were only twenty-nine of the fifty boxes left! Suddenly we saw a misty light, twinkling like stars. In a few moments the chapel was filled with rats who came out of nowhere—that is, seemingly out of the mist! They swarmed over the place all at once. For a moment we stood not knowing what to do, all except Lord Godalming, who was prepared for such an emergency. Rushing over to a great iron-bound door, untried as yet, he turned a key in the lock and swung the door open to the outside air. Then, taking a little silver whistle from his pocket, he blew a low, shrill call. It was answered from the hospital by the yelping of dogs, and after about a minute three terriers came dashing round the corner of the house and into the chapel and attacked the rats, who ran away as quickly as they had come.

Dawn was coming, however, so we locked up the house and departed without danger, quite satisfied with our discovery of the missing boxes.

The hospital was silent when we got back, except for some patient who was screaming away in one of the distant wards.

I came tiptoe into my and Mina's room and found her asleep, breathing rather softly and looking more pale than usual.

Mina Harker's Journal

1 October.—Last night I went to bed when the men had gone. I didn't feel sleepy, thinking over all that has happened since Jonathan and I returned to London.

I can't quite remember how I fell asleep last night. I remember hearing the sudden barking of dogs and a lot of strange sounds from one of the patients' rooms which is below this. And then there was silence, and I got up and looked out of the window. All was dark and quiet, but I watched a thin streak of white mist that crept across the grass towards the hospital. The mist came to the hospital, and I could hear the poor patient below me crying out and fighting something. I was so frightened I crept into bed, and pulled the covers over my head, putting my fingers in my ears. I was not then a bit sleepy, but I must have fallen asleep, for, except dreams, I do not remember anything until the morning, when Jonathan woke me.

One dream was very strange. I was asleep, and waiting for Jonathan to come back. I was very worried about him, but I could not help him, as my feet and hands and brain were weighted, so that they could not move at the usual pace. Then it seemed the air was heavy and cold. I pushed back the covers from my face, and saw a tiny red spark through the fog, which had evidently poured through the window into my room. I closed my eyes, but could still see through my eyelids. (It is wonderful what tricks our dreams will play on us.) The mist came thicker and thicker, till it formed into a pillar of cloud. It had two red eyes, which seemed to shine on me through the fog. The last image of my dream was of a pale white face bending over me out of the mist. Last night tired me more than if I had not slept at all.

Jonathan Harker's Journal

1 October, evening.—I spent today trying to track down the movers who had been hired to transport the missing boxes from the chapel at Carfax. One mover gave me two new addresses, where went twelve of the missing twenty-one boxes. I have more investigating to do tomorrow.

I am tired tonight, and need sleep. Mina is fast asleep, and looks a little too pale; her eyes look as if she had been crying. Poor dear, she worries for me and the others. But we were quite right to keep her out of this dreadful business.

2 October.—I found the mover who transported the remaining nine boxes to a house in Piccadilly. I have located the house, and told my friends, who gathered as usual at Dr. Seward's hospital, of my discovery.

Mina was looking tired and pale. She seems sad at

The dream was of a pale face bending out of the mist.

being left out of our plans. After dinner, I took her to bed, and returned to find the others gathered in the study.

Professor Van Helsing said, "You have done a great day's work, friend Jonathan. We are now on the track of the missing boxes. If we find them all in that house, then our work is near the end. Then we make our final attack, and hunt the wretch to his real death."

I am very sleepy and shall go to bed.

Just one more line. Mina sleeps soundly, and her breathing is regular. She is still too pale, but does not look so worn out as she did this morning.

Dr. Seward's Journal

3 October.—Last night an attendant came bursting into my room and told me that a patient, Renfield, had somehow met with an accident. The attendant had heard him yell, and when he went to him found him lying on his face on the floor, all covered with blood. When I went to examine him, it was clear that he had received some terrible injuries; his face was bruised and bloody, and his back seemed to be broken. But how? I wondered.

"Go to Dr. Van Helsing," I told the attendant, "and ask him to kindly come here at once." The man ran off, and within a few minutes the professor appeared.

The patient was breathing with difficulty. Van Helsing sent the attendant for his surgical instruments. Renfield had a fractured skull and needed immediate surgery.

"We must reduce the pressure of his skull," said Van Helsing, "and get back to normal conditions, as far as that can be." As he was speaking, Arthur and Quincey arrived, asking to be present.

We all watched as Van Helsing removed the blood clot. Renfield, I explained to my friends, is a madman, locked up for his own good. Over the last several months he has taken to eating live flies, spiders and birds. With this strange history in mind, we all shared the dread that somehow Dracula was involved in this attack.

The patient was sinking fast; he might die at any moment. Suddenly his eyes opened, and became fixed in a wild, helpless stare. Then came a sigh of relief. He said, "I have had a terrible dream, and it has left me so weak that I cannot move. What's wrong with my face? It feels all swollen, and it hurts."

"Tell us your dream, Mr. Renfield," said Van Helsing.

"Give me some water, my lips are dry; I shall try to tell you. I dreamed . . . no, I must not lie to myself; it was no dream, but reality. I have something that I must say before I die. It was a few nights ago. I heard the dogs bark behind the hospital. He came up to the window in a mist."

"'He'? Who is 'he'?" asked Van Helsing.

"He is my master," replied Renfield. The professor closed his eyes and nodded, and the madman went on: "He was laughing with his red mouth; his sharp white teeth glinted in the moonlight. I wouldn't ask him to come in at first, though I knew he wanted me to. Then he began promising me things—flies and moths. Then he began to whisper, 'Rats, rats, rats! Hundreds, thousands, millions of them, and every one of them alive! Red blood!' He beckoned me to the closed window. I got up and looked out through the glass, and he raised his hands, and seemed to call out without using any words. A dark mass spread over the grass, coming on like the shape of fire; then he moved the mist to the right and left, and I could see that there were thousands of rats with their eyes blazing red—like his, only smaller. He held up his hand, and they all stopped, and I thought he seemed to be saying, 'All these lives will I give you, and many more and greater, if you will fall down and worship me!' And then a red cloud seemed to close over my eyes, and before I knew what I was doing, I found myself opening the sash and saying to him, 'Come in, Lord and Master!' The rats were all gone, but he slid into the room through the crack in the window, though it was only open an inch wide."

Renfield's voice suddenly faded. After a drink, he went on, having jumped forward in his story. "All day I waited to hear from him, but he did not send me anything, even a fruit fly, and when the moon came up I was angry with him. When he slid in through the crack of the window, and did not even knock, I got mad at him. He sneered at me, and he passed me by as if he owned the whole hospital and I was no one. When he passed by later, I tried to stop him, but I couldn't hold him. He had a new scent about him, that of a woman."

We all started to quiver with fright—we thought of the only woman in the house: Mina!

"When he came tonight, I was ready for him. I saw the mist stealing in, and I grabbed it tight. I thought I was going to win, for I didn't want him to take any more of that woman's life blood. But his eyes burned into me, and I could no longer hold him. He raised me up like a doll and flung me down. There was a red cloud in my eyes, and a noise like thunder, and the mist seemed to steal away under the door."

Van Helsing cried out to us, "We know the worst now. He is here, and we know what he is after. Let us arm ourselves—the same as we were the other night." We all hurried upstairs and took from our rooms the equipment he had passed to us and rushed to the Harkers' door. "Be wise," Van Helsing reminded us, "it is no ordinary enemy that we must deal with."

He turned the handle to their room, but the door did not open. We threw ourselves against it; with a crash it burst open, and we almost fell headlong into the room. What I saw shocked me, and my heart stood still.

The moonlight was so bright that the room was light enough to see. On the bed beside the window lay Jonathan, his breathing heavy as though he were drugged. Kneeling on the near edge of the bed facing outwards was the white-gowned figure of his wife. By her side stood a tall, thin man, dressed in black. His face was turned from us, but we all recognized the Count. With his left hand he held Mrs. Harker's hands;

The Count turned, his eyes red with devilish passion.

his right hand gripped her by the back of the neck, forcing her face down on his bared chest. Her white nightgown was smeared with blood, and a thin stream trickled down the man's chest. The Count turned his face to us, and his eyes flamed red with devilish passion; the white sharp teeth, behind the full lips of the blood-dripping mouth, champed together like those of a wild beast. He threw Mina back on the bed and sprang at us.

The professor, however, was holding out an envelope full of holy wafers, and the Count suddenly stopped. Further and further back he cowered, as we, lifting our crucifixes, advanced. The moonlight suddenly failed, as a great black cloud sailed across the sky; when the gaslight sprang up under Quincey's match, we saw nothing but a faint vapor. This, as we looked, trailed under the door. Van Helsing, Arthur and I moved forward to Mrs. Harker, who by this time had given a scream so wild, so ear-piercing, that it will ring in my ears to my dying day. Her face was ghastly, with a paleness that was highlighted by the blood which smeared her lips and cheeks and chin; from her throat trickled a thin stream of blood; her eyes were mad with terror. Jonathan continued asleep, apparently under the spell of the vampire.

We finally awoke him, and he seemed dazed for a few moments, then he started up. His wife turned to him with her arms outstretched.

"In God's name, what does this mean?" Harker cried out. "Dr. Seward, Dr. Van Helsing, what is it? What has happened? Mina, dear, what is it? What does that blood mean?"

Van Helsing and I tried to calm them both. Jonathan put his arms around Mina and pulled her to him, and for a while she lay there, sobbing.

"And now, Dr. Seward," said Jonathan, "tell me all about it. Too well I can guess it." I told him exactly what happened. As I spoke we saw a bat fly from a window below us—from the room Renfield occupied. The day was dawning. The Count would not be back tonight.

When we returned downstairs, Renfield was dead. We have arranged that one of us is to stay within call of the unhappy couple till we can meet together and arrange about taking action.

Jonathan Harker's Journal

3 October.—When the question began to be discussed as to what should be our next step, the first thing we decided was that Mina should be included in all our planning.

She, for her part, and to my great distress, announced, "If I find in myself—and I shall watch carefully for it—a sign of my harming any of you, I shall kill myself."

I took her in my arms; Van Helsing came over and put his hand on her head, and said, "But, my child, we here will stand between you and death. You must not die. You must not die until the other, who has fouled your sweet life, is truly dead. For if he is still with the Un-Dead, your death would make you as he is. No, you must live! You must struggle to live. Do not die—nor think of death—till this great evil is past."

She shivered, but, thank God, saw his logic, and said, "I promise you, my dear friend, I shall strive to live."

As usual, Van Helsing had thought ahead of everyone else and was prepared with a plan. "It is perhaps well," he announced, "that we decided not to do anything with the earth boxes that lay in the next-door chapel. Had we done so, the Count must have guessed our purpose, but for now he does not know our plans. He probably does not even know that we have the power to sterilize his little hide-outs. We may now track down the last of them. Today, then, is ours. Until the sun sets tonight, that monster must retain whatever form he now has. He cannot melt into thin air nor disappear through cracks in a window. And so we have this day to hunt out all his lairs and sterilize them. Thus we shall, if we have not yet caught and destroyed him, drive him to bay in some place where the catching and the destroying shall be, in time, sure."

Mina took a growing interest in the plans and discussion of how we were to break into the Piccadilly house and the others, and I was glad to see that this was helping her to forget for a time the terrible experience of the night. She was very, very pale—almost ghastly, and so thin that her lips were drawn away, showing her teeth. I did not mention these things, because I did not want to give her new worries; yet it gave my heart a pang to think of what had occurred with poor Lucy when the Count had sucked her blood and she his. As yet there was no sign of the teeth growing sharper, but the time as yet was short, and there was time still for fear.

It was suggested by the professor that after our visit to the estate next to the hospital, we should all enter the house in Piccadilly; that the two doctors and I should remain there, while Lord Godalming and Quincey found the other two lairs across the city and destroyed them. I objected to this plan, for I said that I wanted to stay and protect Mina, but Mina insisted I go; she said that it was the last hope for her that we should all work together.

"Now, my dear friends," announced Van Helsing, "we go forth on our terrible mission. Are we all armed? Then it is well. Now, Madam Mina, you are quite safe here until sunset, and before then we shall return."

We entered the Carfax estate without trouble, and found all the same as before. In the old chapel the great boxes looked just as we had seen them last. Dr. Van Helsing said to us, "And now, my friends, we have a duty here to do. We must sterilize this earth he brought from a distant land." As he spoke, he took from his bag a screwdriver and a wrench, and very soon the top of one of the cases was thrown open. The earth smelled musty. Taking from his bag a piece of holy wafer, he laid it on the earth, and then, shutting down the lid, began to screw it in.

One by one we treated in the same way each of the boxes, and left them looking as we had found them, but in each was a holy wafer. When we closed the door behind us, the professor said, "So much is already

Taking a piece of holy wafer, he laid it on the earth.

done. If it may be that with all the others we can be so successful, then the sunset may bring relief to Madam Mina."

Within a few hours we had arrived and broken into the house in Piccadilly. It smelled as vilely as the Carfax chapel. In the dining room, at the back of the house, we found eight boxes of earth. Eight boxes only out of the

nine we were looking for! Our work was not over, and
would never be until we had found the missing box. In
the dining room we also found title deeds of the houses the Count had bought in London, and other papers.
We found a clothes brush, a brush and comb, and a jug
and basin—the latter containing dirty water which was
reddened as if with blood. Last of all we found a little
heap of keys of all sorts and sizes, marked as belonging
to the other houses. Lord Godalming and Quincey took
with them the keys and set out to destroy the Count's
grave-boxes in those places. The rest of us are awaiting
their return—or the coming of Dracula.

Dr. Seward's Journal

3 October.—Some ninety minutes after Arthur and
Quincey set out, we heard a quiet knock at the hall
door. It made my heart beat loudly. The professor and I
looked at each other, and together we moved out into
the hall. Van Helsing pulled back the latch, having both
his hands ready for action. Fortunately, on the step,
close to the door, we saw our friends. They came quickly in and closed the door behind them, Arthur saying,
"It is all right. We found both places; six boxes in each
and we sterilized them all!"

"There's nothing to do but wait here," said Quincey.
"If, however, he doesn't turn up by five o'clock, we
must start off. It won't do to leave Mrs. Harker alone
after sunset."

Quincey now directed our plan of attack and placed
us each in position. Van Helsing, Harker, and I were just
behind the door, so that if it was opened the professor

could guard it while we two stepped between the incomer and the door. Arthur and Quincey in front stood just out of sight ready to move in front of the window. We waited in suspense.

Several minutes later we all could hear a key softly inserted in the lock of the hall door. Slow, careful steps came along the hall; the Count was evidently ready for some surprise.

Suddenly with a single bound he leaped into the room, past us before any of us could raise a hand to stop him. As the Count saw us, a horrible sort of snarl passed over his face, showing the long and pointed canine teeth. We all advanced on him. Harker pulled out a long knife and made a fierce stab at him. The Count leaped back. I moved forward holding the crucifix and holy wafer in my left hand. I saw the monster cower back. It would be impossible to describe the expression of hate and rage which came over the Count's face. The next instant, he dived under Harker's knife-thrust, and dashed across the room and through the window! Amid the crash of broken glass, he tumbled to the stony yard below.

We ran over to the window sill and saw him spring unhurt from the ground. He crossed the yard, and turned to speak to us: "You think to stop me—*you!* But time is on my side. The women that you love are mine already; and through them you shall yet be mine—my creatures, to do my bidding and to be my jackals! You think you have left me without a place to rest, but I have more. My revenge is just begun!" With a sneer he passed through the gate to the street.

Godalming and Quincey rushed out into the yard, and Harker jumped out of the window to follow the Count. By the time they had got through the gate, there was no sign of him.

It was now late in the afternoon, and sunset was not far off. With heavy hearts we agreed with the professor when he said, "Let us go back to Madam Mina. All we can do just now is done. But we need not despair. There is but one more earth-box, and we must try to find it; when that is done all may yet be well."

When we came back to my house at the hospital, we found Mrs. Harker awaiting us. We told her everything which had passed, and she listened bravely and calmly.

After dinner, the professor fixed up her bedroom against any coming of the vampire, and assured Mrs. Harker that she might rest in peace. When she and Jonathan had gone to bed, Quincey, Godalming, and I arranged that we should sit up, dividing the night between us, and watch over the safety of the poor lady.

Jonathan Harker's Journal

4 October, morning.—During the night I was awakened by Mina. The gray of dawn was coming. "Go, call the professor," she told me. "I want to see him at once."

I rushed and woke him up, and two minutes later he was by Mina's side.

"I want you to hypnotize me!" she said. "Do it before dawn, for I feel that then I can speak freely. Be quick, for the time is short."

He motioned her to sit up in bed, and, looking into her eyes, he passed each of his hands in front of her, up and down, back and forth. Gradually her eyes closed, and she sat still. Then the professor dropped his hands; her eyes opened, but there was a far-away look in them. "Where are you?" asked Van Helsing.

"I do not know," she said with a sad dreaminess.

"What do you see?"

"I can see nothing; it is all dark."

"What do you hear?"

"The lapping of water. It is gurgling by, and little waves."

"Then you are on a ship?"

Gradually her eyes closed, and she sat still.

"Oh, yes!"

"What else do you hear?"

"The sound of men stamping overhead as they run about. There is the creaking of a chain."

"What are you doing?"

"I am still—oh, so still. It is like death!" Her voice faded away, and her eyes closed again.

By this time the sun had risen, and we were in the full light of day. Van Helsing placed his hands on Mina's shoulders, and laid her head down on her pillow. She lay like a sleeping child for a few moments, and then, with a long sigh, awoke and stared in wonder at us. "Have I been talking in my sleep?"

The professor told her what she had spoken, and she said, "Then there is not a moment to lose; it may not be yet too late!"

"That ship," answered Van Helsing, "wherever it was, was weighing anchor. There are many ships leaving your great port of London. Which one do we want? We have, of course, a clue. He has left this morning. He means to escape. He saw that he had but one earth-box left, and a pack of men following him like dogs after a fox. We shall follow him."

"But why need we seek him further, when he is gone away from us?" asked Mina.

"Because, my dear, dear Madam Mina," replied the professor, "now more than ever must we find him, even if we have to follow him to the jaws of Hell!"

"Why?"

"Because he can live for centuries, and you have little time; with that mark upon your throat, if he does not die truly, you are in danger of becoming like him."

I was just in time to catch Mina as she fell forward in a faint.

Dr. Van Helsing, while she recovered, told me, "You are to stay today with dear Mina. We shall go to make our search at the port. He has gone away, back to his castle in Transylvania. He has prepared for this, and that last earth-box was ready to be shipped. We go off now to find what ship, and its route; when we discover that, we shall come back and tell you all. This very creature that we are hunting took hundreds of years to get so far as London; and yet in one day we have been able to drive him out. Take heart, friend Jonathan. This battle is but begun, and in the end we shall win."

Mina Harker's Journal

5 October, 5 P.M.—Our meeting. Dr. Van Helsing report-
ed how he and the others discovered the name of the
boat and its route. The ship is well out to sea. But we
know where to go, and where the box is to land—Varna,
on the Black Sea, east of Transylvania.

I asked him again if it were necessary that they
should pursue the Count, for oh! I dreaded Jonathan
leaving me. The professor became angry: "Yes, it is necessary—necessary—necessary! For your sake, and for

The ship was well out to sea.

the sake of humanity. This monster has done much harm already. He has infected you. Even if he does no more, you have only to die to become like him! This must not be! If we kill him we can save you from such a fate."

Tomorrow at breakfast we are to meet again, and we shall decide how to proceed.

Dr. Seward's Journal

5 October.—When the professor came in, he said, "Friend John, there is something we must talk of alone.—Madam Mina, our poor dear, is changing."

A cold shiver ran through me; I had feared this, and said so.

"Yes," continued Van Helsing. "I can see the characteristics of the vampire coming in her face. Her teeth are somewhat sharper, and at times her eyes are harder. Now, my fear is this: if it be that she can, by our hypnotic trance, tell what the Count sees and hears, is it not possible that he who hypnotized her first, and who has drunk of her very blood and made her drink of his, can compel her mind to tell him what she knows of us?"

I nodded, and the professor went on: "Then we must keep her ignorant of our plans, so she cannot tell what we are doing. This is painful and heart-breaking, but it must be. When today we meet, I must tell her she cannot be part of our committee."

Later.—Mrs. Harker has realized the danger herself; she sent a message saying she thought it better that we should be free to discuss our plans without her.

We went at once into our strategy. Van Helsing told us: "The *Czarina Catherine,* the Count's hired ship, left the Thames yesterday morning. It will take her at least

He said, "There is something we must talk of alone."

three weeks to reach Varna; but we can travel overland to the same place in three days. Thus, in order to be safe, we must leave here on the 17th at latest. But as Varna is unfamiliar to us all, I suggest we go there sooner. Tonight and tomorrow we can get ready, and then we four can set out."

"Four?" said Jonathan.

"Of course," said the professor. "You must remain to take care of your sweet wife!"

Jonathan Harker's Journal

6 October.—Mina woke me early, and asked me to bring Dr. Van Helsing. I thought that it was another occasion for hypnotism, but when the professor came in, she told him, "I must go with you on your journey."

"But why?" asked Van Helsing.

"I am safer with you, and you shall be safer too."

"But why? We go into danger."

"I know. That is why I must go. I can tell you now, while the sun is coming up. I know that when the Count tells me I must go to him, I must. So let me come now of my own free will. I may be of service, since you can hypnotize me and learn details about his travels."

Van Helsing said, "Madam Mina, you are, as always, most wise. You shall come with us, and together we shall succeed."

Now I went with the professor and met with the others. He told us, "Tomorrow morning we shall leave for Varna. There must be no chances lost, and we must be ready to act the instant the ship arrives. That is, we shall board that ship; then, when we have found the box, we shall place a branch of wild rose on it. When it is there, he cannot get out. Then, when we get the chance, and no one is near to see, we shall open the box, and—"

We left London on the morning of the 12th.

"When I see the box," said Quincey, "I shall open it and destroy the monster, though there were a thousand men looking on."

"Bravo, Quincey," said Van Helsing. "But believe me, none of us shall lag far behind you." We shall cut off his head at once and drive a stake through his heart. The professor says that, once we do this, the Count's body will soon turn into dust.

15 October, Varna.—We left London on the morning of the 12th, got to Paris the same night, and took the Orient Express. We traveled night and day, arriving here about five o'clock.

Mina is well, and looks to be getting stronger; her color is coming back. She sleeps a great deal. Before sunrise and sunset, however, she is very wakeful and alert; and it has become a habit for Van Helsing to hypnotize her at such times. He always asks her what she can see and hear. She answers, "I can see nothing; all is dark. But I can hear waves lapping against the ship. The wind is high." It is evident that the Count's ship is still at sea.

We had dinner and went to bed early.

16 October.—Mina's report still the same: lapping waves and rushing water.

24 October.—A whole week of waiting. Mina's morning and evening hypnotic answer is the same: lapping waves, rushing water, creaking masts.

28 October.—We learned today that the Count's ship bypassed Varna and sailed on north to Galatz. I think by now we all expected that something strange would happen.

Dr. Seward's Journal

29 October.—We are on the train from Varna to Galatz. When the usual time came round, Van Helsing hypnotized Mrs. Harker, and she told us, "I can see nothing;

we are still; there are no waves lapping, but only a steady swirl of water running against the ship. I can hear men's voices calling, and the creak of oars. There is tramping of feet overhead, and ropes and chains are dragged along. What is this? There is a gleam of light; I can feel the air blowing upon me." Here she stopped.

She told us, "I can see nothing; we are still."

Van Helsing analyzed her words. "You see, my friends. He has left his earth-box. But he has yet to get on shore. In the night he may lie hidden somewhere, but if he is not carried on shore, or if the ship does not touch it, being a vampire he cannot cross the water by himself to reach land. If the day comes before he can get on shore, then he cannot escape. We may then arrive in time; for if he does not escape tonight, we shall come on him in the daytime, boxed up and at our mercy."

Mina Harker's Journal

30 October, Galatz.—We arrived too late. The men are leaving to pursue the Count, whose box, we have learned from port officials, has been transported to a boat on the river leading to Transylvania. Van Helsing took my hands and said, "This time we may succeed. Our enemy is at his most helpless: if we can come on him by day, on the water, our task will be over. He has a head start, but he is powerless to hurry, as he may not leave his box or those who carry him may suspect what it is they are carrying; for them to suspect would be to prompt them to throw him in the water, where he would perish. Now, men, to our council of war. For, here and now, we must plan what each shall do."

"I shall hire a small, speedy steamboat and follow him up the river," said Lord Godalming.

"And I shall hire horses to follow on the riverbank, if he should reach land," said Quincey Morris.

"Good!" said the professor. "But neither of you should go alone. There must be force to overcome force, if need be; the Gypsies carrying him are strong and rough."

He assigned Jonathan to go with Lord Godalming, while Dr. Seward would accompany Quincey. "Be not afraid for Madam Mina," Van Helsing continued, "she will be in my care. I will take Madam Mina right into the heart of the enemy's country. While the creature is in his box, we shall go on the track where Jonathan went—from Bistritz over the Borgo Pass, and find our way to the castle of Dracula. Here, Madam Mina's hypnotic power will surely help, and we shall find our way after the first sunrise to that dreadful place. There is much to be done, and other places to be cleansed, so that that nest of snakes is destroyed."

Later.—It took all my courage to say goodbye to my darling Jonathan. We may never meet again.

It took all my courage to say goodbye to Jonathan.

31 October.—Arrived at Veresti at noon. The professor tells me that this morning at dawn he could hardly hypnotize me, and that all I could say was: "Dark and quiet." We have something more than 70 miles before us in a carriage.

1 November.—At sunset the professor hypnotized me, and he says that I answered as usual: "Darkness, lapping water, and creaking wood." So our enemy is still on the river.

Abraham Van Helsing's Journal

4 November.—We got to the Borgo Pass just after sunrise yesterday morning. Madam Mina awoke, and as if some guiding power were in her, she pointed to a road, and said, "This is the way."

So we came down this road, and when we came to other roads, the horses, also seeming bewitched, knew which way to go. We went on for hours and hours. But Madam Mina slept and slept. In the late afternoon I awoke her. I keep trying to hypnotize her, but I cannot. When the sun went down, Madam Mina laughed. She looks better in health than I ever saw her. I am amazed, and nervous. I lit a fire, and she prepared food while I undid the horses and set them to feed. Then when I returned to the fire, she had my supper ready. She told me she had eaten already—that she was so hungry she could not wait. I did not like those words. I ate, and then we set out the blankets by the fire. I told her to sleep, while I watched. But I had started to doze, when suddenly I remembered that I was to watch, and I found her lying quietly, but awake, and looking at me with bright, bright eyes.

At sunrise, she fell asleep and would not wake up. I lifted her up and placed her in the carriage. She is still asleep, and she looks in her sleep more healthy than before. And I do not like that. I am afraid.

5 November.—All yesterday we traveled, ever getting closer to the mountains. Madam Mina slept and slept— I could not awaken her, even for food. I began to fear that the fatal spell of the place was upon her, infected as she is by the vampire. "Well," I said to myself, "if it be that she sleeps all day, it shall also be that I do not sleep at night." I fell asleep in the afternoon as the carriage went on, the horses choosing the course. When I awoke, just before sunset, Madam Mina was still asleep. I stopped the carriage, and managed to wake her up, and again tried to hypnotize her, but it did not work. The sun went down in the snowy peaks, and I took out the horses and fed them in what shelter I could find. Then I made a fire, and near it I made Madam Mina sit. She was awake and more weirdly charming than ever, sitting comfortably amid her blankets. I got the food ready, but she would not eat, simply saying that she was not hungry. But I did eat, needing to be strong. Then, with fear of what might happen, I drew a ring around Madam Mina's place, and around the ring I placed some of the holy wafer, and I broke it very fine so that all was well guarded. She sat still all the time— as still as the dead. When I drew near, she clung to me, and she shook from head to foot.

Soon the horses began to scream, and tore at their ropes, till I came to them and quieted them. Many times through the night did I have to go to them. At midnight the fire began to die, and I was about to gather more wood for it; there was snow falling about us. But then it seemed that through the snow and mist I could see the shape of women in long white garments. The horses whinnied in terror. I stayed within the circle. I feared for my dear Madam Mina when these ghostly figures drew near and circled round. I looked at her, but she sat calm, and when I would have stepped out to get wood, she held me back, and whispered, in a dreamy voice, "No, no, do not go outside the circle! Here you are safe!"

"But it is for you that I fear!" I said.

"Fear for me! There are none safer in all the world

from them than I am," she said. The figures of mist and snow came closer, but keeping ever outside the circle of holy wafer. Then they began to materialize, till there were before me in actual flesh what must have been the same three women that Jonathan saw in the room, when they would have kissed and bit his throat. They had bright hard eyes, sharp teeth, and full red lips. They smiled at poor Madam Mina; they laughed, twining their arms, and, pointing at her, said, "Come, sister. Come to us!"

They laughed and said, "Come, sister. Come to us!"

I was glad to see that Mina had terror in her eyes and did not make a move toward them. Finally the red of dawn came through the snowy gloom. When that beautiful sun began to climb the horizon, life came back to me again. The horrid women melted away into the whirling mist and snow.

With the dawn coming, I turned to Madam Mina to hypnotize her, but she now lay in a sudden and deep sleep. I fear yet to go. I have made the fire and have seen the horses; they are all dead. I will strengthen myself with breakfast for my hike to the castle.

Later.—When I left Madam Mina sleeping within the circle of holy wafers, I took my way up the mountain to the castle. I brought a blacksmith's hammer, with which I broke off the doors from their hinges so that I would not be trapped within. By memory of Jonathan's diary I found my way to the chapel, for I knew that there was where my work lay. The air was disgusting, which at times made me dizzy. I heard afar off the howl of wolves.

I knew there were at least three graves to find— graves in which the women lay. I searched and searched, and found one of them. She lay in her vampire sleep, so full of life and beauty that I shuddered as though I had come to do murder. Yes, I seemed paralyzed by her beauty to do what I had come to do. Then I heard from a distance, down the mountain, a long, low wail of woe—the voice of my dear Mina. So I braced myself again to my horrid task, and found by wrenching away the tomb lids the other two women. Amid their tombs there was one larger and grander than the rest. On it was but one word: DRACULA.

This then was the Un-Dead home of the king vampire. Before I began to restore these women to their dead selves through my awful work, I laid in Dracula's tomb some of the holy wafer, and so prevented him from it, Un-Dead, forever.

Then began my terrible task. Had it been but one, it would have been comparatively easy. But three! Had I not thought of my dear Mina, I could not have gone on.

I could not have endured the horrid screeching as the stake drove home; the writhing body, the lips of bloody foam. But it is over! And the poor souls; I can pity them now as I think of them, each in her full sleep of death. Hardly had my knife severed the head of each, before the whole body began to melt away and crumble into dust.

Before I left the castle I so fixed its entrances that never more can the Count enter there.

When I returned and stepped into the circle in which Madam Mina slept, she woke from her sleep, and, see-ing me, cried out, "Let us go meet my husband! I know he is coming here."

And so we hurriedly walk eastward to meet our friends.

Mina Harker's Journal

6 November.—It was late in the afternoon when the pro-fessor and I took our way towards the east from where I knew Jonathan was coming. It was steeply downhill. About a mile down we looked back and saw where the clear line of Dracula's castle cut the sky. We saw it in all its magnificence, perched a thousand feet on the sum-mit of a sheer cliff. We could hear the distant howling of wolves. The professor then found us a spot upon a boulder where, out of sight, we could await our friends and the Gypsies carting Dracula. He brought out blan-kets and furs to make a snug nest for me.

Soon we could see straight in front of us a group of men on horses hurrying along. In the midst of them was a long wagon. On the wagon was a large box. My heart leaped as

I saw it, for I felt that the end was coming. The evening was almost upon us, and I knew that at sunset the thing, which was till then imprisoned in the box, would have new freedom and could take any form and escape.

Then the professor shouted, "Look! Two horsemen follow fast, coming up from the south. It must be Quincey and John. Take the spy-glass and look!" He handed the glass to me and I looked. The two men were indeed Mr. Morris and Dr. Seward. I knew, however, that Jonathan was not far off; looking around, I saw on the north side two other men riding at break-neck speed. It was Jonathan and Lord Godalming. They, too, were chasing the horsemen with the wagon.

We knew that before long the sun would set. They were all riding hard and approaching us. They were unaware of our watching. Perhaps if the Gypsies eluded our friends, the professor and I could surprise and stop them. Suddenly two voices shouted out, "Halt!" The Gypsies slowed down, and at that instant Lord Godalming and Jonathan dashed up at one side of them and Dr. Seward and Mr. Morris on the other. The leader of the Gypsies, waving his gun, told his fellows to go on. At that moment our friends raised their rifles, and Dr. Van Helsing and I rose behind the boulder and pointed our weapons. Seeing that they were surrounded, the Gypsies stopped.

The Gypsy leader, however, pointed to the sun—now close down on the hilltops—and then to the castle, and said something which I did not understand. All four men of our group dashed towards the wagon, but the Gypsies ran to block them.

Jonathan, however, was unstoppable; he knocked through the Gypsies and leaped onto the cart, seizing the great box and heaving it off the wagon and onto the ground. The Gypsies stabbed at Mr. Morris as he rushed to help Jonathan, and he was bleeding terribly. Even so, he pried off one end of the chest's lid while Jonathan cracked open the other end; the nails screeched as they were pulled out, and the top of the box was thrown back.

The Gypsies finally gave up and watched. The sun was almost down on the mountaintops. I saw the Count lying within the box upon the earth. He was deathly pale, like wax, and his red eyes glared with hatred. As I looked, his eyes saw the sinking sun.

But, at that instant, came the sweep and flash of Jonathan's knife. I shrieked as I saw it cut through the throat, while at the same moment Mr. Morris's knife plunged into the heart.

It was like a miracle; before our very eyes the whole body crumbled into dust and passed from sight.

The Gypsies turned, without a word, and rode away as if for their lives.

Mr. Morris, who had sunk to the ground, held his hand to his side, but the blood gushed through his fingers. I ran down to him; so did the two doctors.

He smiled in his last moments and said, "I am only too happy to have been of service! It is worth it to die, for the curse of Dracula has passed away!"